SHROUD₄

From
Shroud Publishing LLC

You are holding a limited edition small press publication in your hands. This book is a result of hard work and creative effort. Enjoy it and celebrate the possibility of all things.

Designed and Printed in the USA

SP
Shroud Publishing

www.shroudmagazine.com

First Edition
First Printing December 5, 2008
Copyright 2008 Shroud Publishing
All Rights Reserved

The individual copyrights of the respective authors herein reverted back to the original copyright holder upon publication.

Cover Art by Martin Blanco
http://www.martblanco.com/

ISBN: 978-0-9801870-9-0

Shroud Publishing LLC
121 Mason Rd.
Milton, NH 03851
www.shroudmagazine.com

Shroud 4   The Journal of Dark Fiction and Art

Shroud 4 The Journal of Dark Fiction and Art

Shroud 4, Fall 2008

SHROUD 4
The Journal of Dark Fiction and Art

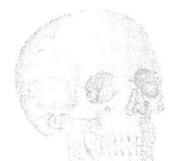

Shroud 4
Fall 2008

Publisher
Shroud Publishing LLC

Editor
Timothy P. Deal

Assistant Editor
Robert Canipe
Christa M. Miller

Marketing
Jennifer N. Deal

Layout and Design
Brian Hanson
Dale Mythito

Contributing Editors
I.E. Lester
Norman Rubenstein
Steve Vernon
DL Snell

Contributing Artists
Martin Blanco

Cover Art
Martin Blanco

ISSN
1940-7025

Copyright (c) 2008 by Shroud Publishing LLC. Individual works are copyright (c) 2008 by their respective creators. All rights reserved.

Fiction
A GRAVE AFFAIR, Jason Keene	6
GLACIAL MELT, Sara King	12
A NAZI MEDICAL OFFICER'S TALE, Kurt Bachard	18
PRINCE ABBADON AND THE CHOSEN, Robert T. Canipe	24
PET CEMETERY, Linda Courtlans	27
ON THE MOUNTAIN, John Mantooth	29
INEXTINGUISHABLE, Jessica Lynn Gardner	33
THE CONTRACT, William A. Veselik	35
OUTSIDE THE LINES, Tim Waggoner	39
THREE GRAVES, Blu Gilliand	47
SKETCH OF A RUIN, Michael J. Deluca	51
OFFERINGS, Desmond Warzel	59
LAURA, J.F. Gonzalez	60
PRIMING PAMELA, Lauren Salkin	73
THE BULB, Ernestor Burden	84
LOVE AND WAR, John C. Caruso	90
TEMPLE, Gerard Houarner	103
ALONE, Edward Fleming	111

Nonfiction/Columns
THE DEVIL CAME DOWN TO JERSEY, Steve Vernon	8
BRAM STOKER, I.E. Lester	20
DARK EFFIGIES: MARTIN BLANCO, Tim Deal	69
DL SNELL'S MARKET SCOOPS, DL Snell	94
SPECIALTY PRESS SHOWCASE, Norm Rubenstein	101

Books
THE DARKEST EVENING OF THE YEAR by Dean Koontz	77
QUEEN OF BLOOD by Bryan Smith	78
INSTITUTIONAL MEMORY by Gary Frank	78
RAVENOUS by Ray Garton	79

Film
THE CHANGELING, by Marie O'Regan	81

From The Editor:
The Joy of Fear
And the Gnashing of Teeth

The last couple of months have been crazy and exciting—both on the personal and professional fronts. On the personal front, our new son, Seamus, has begun daycare and seems to be growing by leaps every day. It is absolutely amazing (and wonderful) how much time an infant takes up of your day. Then the election, which was fraught with drama at every turn and introduced some new and interesting personalities to national politics. On the Shroud front we signed a national distribution deal with Ingram periodicals and are looking forward to being able to share these wonderful stories with a much wider audience. The deal is brand new and will take a couple months to sort out, but we are very confident that the quality of our content will propel us forward to major book retailers across North America. I would humbly ask that the next time you are at Barnes and Noble, go ask about Shroud; build a buzz; help us generate excitement about dark literature and art.

Also on the Shroud front, we had the absolute pleasure of attending the Context 21 convention in Columbus, Ohio. With all sincerity I would have to say that the guest, attendees, and co-ordinators were some of the best people on the planet. We enjoyed the hell out of ourselves, and the Shroud Party was no less than legendary. I am compelled to throw a quick shout out to some folks that were helpful, supportive, or just downright cool: Mark Wholley, Scott McCoy, Sheldon Higdon and his beautiful wife, Dan and Jackie Gamber from Meadowhawk Press, Greg Hall and the Choate Road Crew, and our writer friends that were nice enough to offer book signings in our suite, Brian Keene, Gary Braunbeck, D. Harlan Wilson, J.F. Gonzalez, Tim Waggoner, Sheldon Higdon, and Joseph McGee. I know I have left a few of you out, and I apologize, but a big thanks to everyone at Context, you know who you are!

Mark Wholley mans the Shroud Booth at Context 21

I'd also like to announce that we have added a few new columnists to Shroud including talented authors and veterans of the Horror genre Steve Vernon, Norman Rubenstein, DL Snell, and Michael Knost. Steve's column first appeared in issue Two and features "real life" hauntings, while Norman will write about new small press publishers, DL will discuss markets, and Michael will spotlight up and coming writers within dark literature. Shroud is delighted to have them on board and we are certain you will be thrilled with their contributions.

Lastly, and certainly not least, we are happy to include the third Photo Flash Fiction Contest results, as featured on MySpace. This issue, instead of clumping all of the honorable mentions and winner together, we've decided to spread the stories out throughout the issue in order to better showcase their individual merits. Please let us know what you think. This issue, the contest photo (as seen below) depicts a lonely grouping of headstones located in rural New Hampshire. We received scores of entries, many of which were well crafted and entertaining. Our winner was Jessica Gardner, who captured the image perfectly in her chilling little tale Inextinguishable.

Scott McCoy, Mark Wholley, and Tim Deal eager to serve at the Context 21 Shroud Party

Honorable Mentions:

1. OFFERINGS, by Desmond Warzel
2. ALONE, by Edward Fleming
3. PET CEMETERY, by Linda Courtland
4. A GRAVE AFFAIR, by Jason Keene
5. THREE GRAVES, by Blu Gilliand

Ms. Gardner will receive paid publication in this issue as well as a book and DVD prize package.

So once again, sit back and enjoy another jam-packed issue of Shroud, filled with horrifying and thought-provoking tales of suspense and the supernatural.

The lonely graves for the 3rd Shroud Photo Flash Fiction Contest

Tim Deal, November 2008

Shroud 4   The Journal of Dark Fiction and Art

Flash Fiction Contest Honorable Mention

A GRAVE AFFAIR

JASON KEENE

Hannah sat upon the aged stone steps and waited. The evening was drawing in and the last rays of the autumn sun cast shadows across the forest floor.

Daniel finally emerged from the thick overgrowth of the path, a blanket tucked haphazardly under his arm, carrying a Coleman lantern.

"A little morbid even for you, don't you think?" he asked as he neared the clearing, nodding in the direction of the four weathered headstones erected in a row behind her.

"Your wife doesn't know you're here?" Hannah questioned, rising from the steps and seductively striding over to him while biting on the tip of her black nail polish with a look of youthful innocence.

"She doesn't have a clue, baby," he grinned, opening his arms to welcome the embrace of his young mistress.

Since meeting Hannah at the club downtown last month, Daniel had met up with her on several occasions for no-ties sex. His wife had no idea the affair was going on and he intended to keep it that way. Hannah had been an animal when he held her up and pinned her back against the wall of the school gym during the Homecoming game. Daniel had hit his mid-life stride, and this young tart was the solution to his sex crisis.

"Good." She smiled through the sheen of her purple lipstick before slowly dropping to her knees. "Nobody will come looking for you."

Grasping a thick piece of wood from the ground, Hannah rose up at an angle and struck Daniel across the side of the head. He was on the ground and unconscious before he could even react.

Daniel awoke in total darkness. His head was still ringing from the blow, and he fumbled blindly through debris as he tried to stand.

"Is that you down there, loverboy?" Hannah called out from somewhere above him, her voice distant.

"Where the hell am I?" Daniel called out, echoing in darkness.

"Well, the way I see it, we've been seeing each other for about a month now," she said, sitting atop the large slab of rock that hid the entrance to Daniel's earthen cell below. "I think it's about time you met the family."

The earth surrounding Daniel's chamber shifted, and he fell backwards. Groping in the darkness, he could make out the smooth rounded edges and long slender shafts of the debris scattered around him--bones. The rancid scent of wet earth and decay caught his nostrils as more movement came from the darkness around him. Something leathery and cold gripped his ankle, then his throat. His fists beat wildly at his attackers while his muffled screams vibrated the hollow cavern below the stone structure.

Hannah strolled over to the last grave and brushed the dirt and leaves from its lettering. She had always hated when the elements got the best of her tombstone and covered up her name.

I hope they leave a nibble for me this time, she thought.

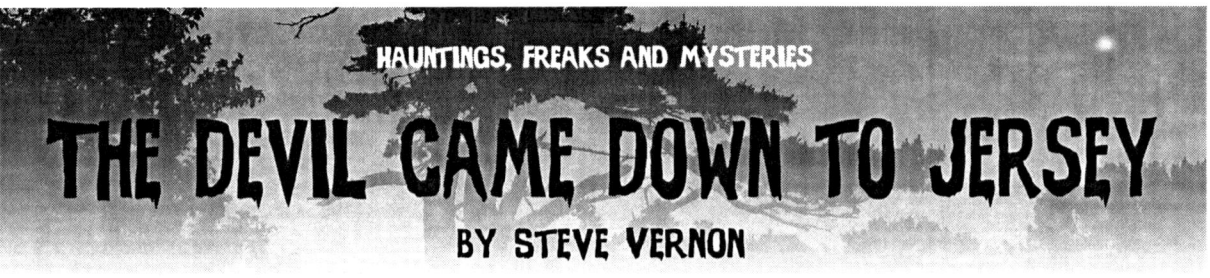

HAUNTINGS, FREAKS AND MYSTERIES
THE DEVIL CAME DOWN TO JERSEY
BY STEVE VERNON

Kangaroo horse, king-o-wing, cowbird, flying hoof, the Leeds Devil – all names for a beast more commonly known as the Jersey Devil.

"(It) appeared to be a large crane...emitting a glow like a firefly. Its head resembled that of a ram with curled horns and its long thick neck was thrust forward in flight. It had long thin wings and short legs, the front legs shorter than the hind."
- E.W. Minster, Postmaster of Bristol
January 1909

"(It had the) body of a man, head of a cow, large bat wings, big feet and if flew up in the air cutting off the tops of trees."
- Howard Marcey and John Huntzinger
July 1930

"A large winged creature with a horse-like head and bird-like legs."
- Joseph Bonaparte
Brother of Napoleon and ex-king of Spain
1820

The beast has as many descriptions as names, but what is the origin of this strange savage monster? There are many tales. This is the most popular.

The Curse of Mother Leeds

Early in the 18th century Mother Leeds lay in labour in her candle-lit shanty, giving birth to her thirteenth child, being aided by an ancient midwife.

"I don't want it," she said. "Take the goddamn thing away."

"How can a mother curse her child?" the midwife wondered.

"I'm tired of children," Mother Leeds snarled. "I wish to hell it was born a devil."

The moonless night sky tore itself apart a snarl of thunder and lightning. Mother Leeds groaned and heaved and gave sudden violent birth.

"A handsome boy-child," the midwife declared.

"A devil," Mother Leeds swore.

At those words the child's body elongated hideously. The child's tiny feet thickened and blunted into twin cloven hooves. The cherub-like features lengthen into heavy horse jaws. A pair of taut leather bat wings unfurled from his shoulder blades and a thick forked tail sprouted from the base of his distorted spinal column.

The Jersey Devil was born.

Before you could say "Godzilla ate Tokyo," the monster tore through the shanty, devouring all twelve Leeds children. Some say it ate the mother and midwife, too. It flew up the chimney and into the night – doubtless in search of some Gaviscon.

The Hunt is On

Since then the Devil have hunted the beast, shot at it, ran over it, tried to exorcise it, debunked it, and even fired a cannon at it. Yet year after year folks continue to report devil-sightings.

May, 2007 – a young Freehold woman spotted a "large beast with bat-like wings".

August, 2007 – a young man spotted a "gargoyle-like creature with partially spread bat wings perched in a tree".

January, 2008 – A Litchfield, Pennsylvania man witnessed the creature come screaming out of his barn.

The sightings continue to pile up in the Jersey area. Is it mass hysteria, a series of pranks, or is there indeed, something out there.

The Jersey Devil only knows.

The Atmosphric hunting grounds of Jersey--home to the Jersey Devil. Seen as late as January of this year. (S. Vernon)

GET GRUESOME!

Special Signed & Numbered Limited Edition of Gregory Lamberson's Novel JOHNNY GRUESOME from Bad Moon Books
Featuring an Introduction by Jeff Strand and Six Full Color Illustrations by Zach McCain

"Bold and trashy in all the right ways, Johnny Gruesome is a book (and a villain) you won't soon forget."
-- Lee Thomas, author of PARISH DAMNED and THE DUST of WONDERLAND

"Johnny Gruesome has a frightening sense of detail that makes it all the more horrific -- it's a gruesome ride that you can't stop reading." -- Gunnar Hansen, Leatherface

ALSO AVAILABLE

The 'GRUESOME' Rock CD By Giasone and Marcy Italiano!
The Johnny Gruesome DEATH MASK!
The GRUESOME Mini-Movie starring Misty Mundae!
And the On-Line JOHNNY GRUESOME Comic Book!

Visit www.JohnnyGruesome.com

Bart Willard: "Oracle"

www.bartwillard.com

GLACIAL MELT

BY SARA KING

Hanna's sister was prattling on about global warming as they hiked along the edge of the Matanuska Glacier, insisting that the dirty wall of ice before them was proof, when Hannah saw the skull.

At first, Hannah thought it was a bumpy white stone sunk amidst the silt and wildflowers, but when she and Amy moved closer to the wall of ice, she quickly realized that the divots in the rock were actually eye sockets filled with sand.

"Aren't those pretty?" Amy asked, pointing to the tiny clumps of dwarf fireweed shivering against the cold glacial breeze. She had not yet seen the skull, or if she had, she had dismissed it as just another ice-rounded stone. She squatted beside a clump and began to pick them, her left knee almost touching the skull.

Hannah touched her sister's shoulder, unable to tear her eyes from the empty eye sockets. "Amy..." she began.

Amy grinned up at her from her handful of wildflowers. "We can put them in the tent tonight."

Staring at the skull, Hannah realized that she wanted nothing more than to turn and run, and report the remains to authorities. Some instinct told her the poor soul now resting in the silt and wildflowers had not died a happy death. In fact, more than anything, the word murder was chilling the edges of her subconscious.

"I think we should go back to the car," Hannah said. "Camp somewhere else."

Amy's girlish face looked stricken. "But it took all day to get out here." She jiggled the huge pack she carried and added, "And my back hurts."

Hannah's back also hurt, but her hip now burned where the .44 revolver rested against her thigh, brought along in case of a bear attack.

Afterward, Hannah couldn't say why she didn't tell Amy of the skull. Perhaps the gun left her with a false sense of security. Or the childish innocence in her sister's face as she squatted beside it amongst the wildflowers, oblivious, had overpowered her fears--or maybe she was simply too tired to care. Amy was right... they had hiked all day to get there, from ten o'clock that morning to almost eight o'clock that night, the sun was still gloriously high overhead, and she had a gun big enough to blow away Bigfoot.

So Hannah said nothing, not wanting to frighten her innocent little sister, who had paled and argued against bringing the gun the moment she saw Hannah carrying it, claiming bears were 'harmless creatures.' Hannah knew it was merely a gentle soul seeing similar qualities in everything around her, and had pretended to put the gun back into the trunk, then strapped it on under her jacket when Amy wasn't looking.

Now the gun seared her hip as they hiked another five minutes, found a dry sandbar, and set up camp. As soon as they had the tent prepared, Hannah dropped the bomb that she had, in fact, brought along the .44.

Amy was pissed. She stalked off under the excuse she was 'searching for firewood,' and Hannah had to putter around the campsite for an hour by herself while she waited for her sister to cool down. When Amy finally returned, still not speaking, Hannah left the gun on the bed, told her little sister to use it if she needed it, and went off for some quiet time of her own.

Morbidly, she hiked back to the skull with her digital camera, telling herself the pictures were for the authorities and not her own perverse interest.

Once Hannah had walked further beyond the glacial wall than she remembered seeing it, she doubled back, scanning the ground for the telltale brightness of bone, thinking she had walked past it.

The skull was no longer there.

She found Amy's distinctive circular tread leading up to a thick patch of dwarf fireweed, and when she drew closer, she saw the depression where the base of the skull had sunk into the silt, and the sand that was still moist from its removal.

Around it, leading off toward the glacier, was a man's footprints.

Immediately, Hannah's mind

was filled with images of stalkers and insane hermits, but she quickly put a rein on her fears. It was probably just some sicko hiker who decided to take it home as a souvenir.

And yet, when Hannah glanced back in the direction of their tent, her hair prickled in her pores. She had to fight the urge to run back to Amy.

She's all right, Hannah thought. *Gathering firewood*.

Yet she saw no movement around the tent. When she squinted, she could not make out Amy's form on the nearby mountain slope, nor on the rugged ice above her.

Amy is wearing red, Hannah realized. Her unease jumped a notch. Amongst the grays and greens and browns, a red jacket was impossible to miss.

"Amy?" Hannah shouted in the direction of the tent. She could see it cresting a rise almost four hundred yards away. The tent flap was open, and Amy was not inside.

Amy did not answer.

"Amy!" Hannah shouted, trying not to sound panicked, in case her sister was still sulking. She took a couple steps toward the tent, stopping suddenly.

Something was watching her from the ice. Hannah could see it, shadowed by a cleft in the glacier's face. She peered more closely, her brain trying frantically to attribute it to a deformity in the ice, a trick of the light--anything other than a man standing there, watching her.

The eyes shattered such whimsy.

They were bright blue, contrasting against a face darkened and wrinkled by the elements, hidden above a dirty white medical mask and tattered earmuffs.

And they were fixed on her. Utterly motionless. Waiting.

More on impulse than rational thought, Hannah bolted. She flung herself at the tent, her instincts telling her she had to reach Amy and the .44 revolver now, or both her and her sisters' skulls were going to join the other one, collecting glacial melt each spring.

The stranger gave chase.

Hannah heard him behind her, his feet thudding methodically against the sand as he caught up. She was tall and lanky for a girl, but she'd never been in track, never exercised more than a few times a month. She was the slower of the two.

He's going to catch me. Seeing the distance still between herself and the tent, Hannah knew this was true. Screaming out Amy's name, she spun, whipped her arm around, and punched at the stranger's throat.

His too-blue eyes widened, but he ducked at the last minute and her blow glanced off the side of his neck. Then he was on her, dragging her down to the ground. In that one, brutal instant, Hannah knew she was going to die. It was her sister, however, that occupied her thoughts.

Amy.

The stranger had gagged her and was wrenching her arms behind her back as she screamed into the rags when Hannah saw the .44 secured to his hip.

Her .44.

She redoubled her struggles at that point, and Hannah's last, terrified thought before the stranger began slamming a stone into the back of her head was of her sister. It was a desperate quailing inside of her, a fear greater than death itself. Then, nothing.

* * *

Allen stopped dead in his tracks. He scanned the craggy crevices of silt-layered ice, felt the cool wind tickle his hair under the bands of his medical mask, tasted the pure Alaskan air on his tongue. For a moment, he feared that someone had found the girl, and that what had stopped him had been the predator's instinct, the inner voice that told him an intruder had stumbled upon his cache.

But when he glanced back over his shoulder, the landscape was calm. Peaceful. The silt-laden runoff trickled a few yards below the cave he'd made in the ice, undisturbed by passing feet. The girls' tent, which he had collapsed and hidden, no longer marred the landscape. No other hikers invaded his secluded haven, a sheltered nook between a wall of ice and a slope of stone. Wildflowers quivered in the glacier-cooled breeze, clinging to the deposits of land only recently uncovered by the glacier's receding footprint.

Officially, Allen was dead. His bush plane had gone down three years ago, ground to dust inside the crevices of the great ice monster. Rescuers had spent weeks looking for him in another part of the state, never suspecting that Allen did not have a desire to be found.

Never suspecting that the pilot had also not been killed in the crash, but rather, by Allen's hands, as they thrust him into a ravine.

Allen now wore the pilot's teeth on a thong around his neck, not because he believed in some primitive idea of capturing the spirit of his prey--Marty Jones had been red-faced, balding, and approximately big enough to fill the 500-pound weight restrictions on his tiny bush plane, hardly a challenging opponent except for the mere fact his bulk made shoving him over the edge more difficult--but because by keeping them on his person it would be harder for authorities to identify the fat bastard, should they ever find his body amidst the dwarf fireweed trembling along the glacier's edge.

Allen, on the other hand, would never be found. He'd spent ten years preparing for his escape, two years carving out and supplying his haven, and three months orchestrating Marty's flight patterns so that rescuers thought they'd taken their usual route north, instead of due east out of Anchorage.

And, as both Marty's bloated corpse and the bright-eyed young blonde bound and gagged in his ice cave could both attest to, Allen was ready to do anything to protect his freedom.

Allen giggled through his mask. He delighted in watching the fears build and coalesce on their faces, found joy in their tiny whimpers as they refused to voice them aloud, as if speaking them would somehow bring them to life.

Allen tested the density of the soil by scuffing it with his foot, scouting a suitable place to bury the bodies, for when he got bored of them. He didn't think that would take long—something about the women had reminded him of the flowers that had sprouted around Marty's bloated corpse earlier that spring.

He hated flowers.

Flowers meant pollen, and pollen--that disgusting, spermy substance that crawled into the nose and down the throat and worked its way into the glands and tissues of the unwary—pollen was why he'd abandoned the disgusting clefts of civilization for rugged waves of ice. Out here, amidst the cold, rippling desert, pollen held no sway. Near the middle of the glacier, Allen could actually remove his face gear without fear of infestation.

But for now, with spring in full bloom around him and an unavoidable need to eat, Allen had had to cope with the disgusting substance while he resupplied himself for the blessed reprieve of winter.

Unfortunately, being this close to the edge of the glacier always carried with it a risk of being seen.

Allen took a deep breath of the glacial breeze and smiled down at the woman he'd left hogtied among the driftwood, wide-eyed and gasping through her gag. She was beautiful. The face of an angel, with a fiery look to her eyes that told of a strong inner spirit.

He bent down and gently removed the facemask he'd affixed over her mouth and nose. "Are you comfortable?" he asked.

"What did you do to my sister?" the woman whimpered.

"Nothing, yet," Allen said. "Calm down. I'm not going to hurt you."

The woman began to cry in grateful helplessness. Her large breasts rose and fell as she tried not to hyperventilate. Allen drew out his knife, considered untying her and coercing her into removing her bright red jacket, shit, pants, and undergarments, then just decided he'd cut them off of her later.

"Please don't hurt my sister," she whimpered. "I don't care what you do to me, but please don't hurt her."

"I won't," Allen said. Smiling, he plunged the knife into her belly and slit it open, enjoying the startled look on the girl's face before she started screaming.

* * *

As soon as the stranger left, Hannah began to struggle, twisting her wrists with enough force to break the skin, but the bones in her hands betrayed her. She remained snugly in place, hands and feet remaining where the madman had staked them to the ice.

He was going to kill her. Hannah had known it the moment she'd seen him standing in a crack in the glacier wall, watching her with ice-blue eyes above a white medical breathing mask. Something about the coldness there chanted *murder*.

Then she heard the scream. Thin, high, it was like a terrified child crying for its mother. Hannah thrashed against the ice, frantically calling her sister's name through the gag the stranger had stuffed into her mouth.

Amy. Oh, God, *Amy!* What was the bastard doing to her?!

Hannah screamed in frustration, but the ice would not yield. She could only slam her head against the wall and sob in helplessness as her sister's cries lessened, until she was leaning forward, straining to hear them, willing to hear them.

Afterwards, when her sister's pitiful cries had finally died, Hannah heard footsteps outside. She screamed her fury against the dirty, rag-stuffed medical mask he had used to muffle her cries and tried again to yank her wrists free from the hook he'd hammered into the ice above her, to no avail.

Hannah's heart thundered and a bitter cold formed in the pit of her stomach, a fear that left her feeling every ounce of her vulnerability as rising terror slid into the crevices of her brain.

The footsteps moved beyond the cave entrance, casting only a shadow along the rim before passing on. One moment, two, the stranger waited. Hannah heard short, snapping sounds in the silence that followed, like strands of hair breaking. She held her breath, waiting for the unworldly scratching of boots against ice as Death made its way to her resting place.

When they came, she was so paralyzed with fear she could only hold herself up against the pull of the stakes, eyes riveted to the entrance.

The man that entered was not the man who had run her down on the sandbar. This one was huge, a hulking giant with a deceptively sweet face. Yet he seemed neither surprised nor angered by her appearance in the cave, and the mere fact he made no move to untie her meant he was in league with the monster. Hannah felt a part of herself die inside as he moved closer, a fistful of blazing pink dwarf fireweed clenched in one fat fist. She trembled as he bent down, found the zipper of her jacket, and began pulling it down, exposing the tight tank-top she wore underneath.

"Please," she tried to say, but it was muffled by the gag. The stranger ignored her. Hannah stiffened as his big hand reached under her tank-top, grazing a breast as he pulled it down. She shuddered, tried to pull away, but his face showed absolutely no concern for her condition.

He's going to rape me.

The horrible realization left Hannah trembling with helplessness. She wanted to shout, wanted to cry, but she could only watch with horror as her would-be rapist fumbled with her clothing.

But, upon lifting her tank-top, the big stranger dumped his fistful of dwarf fireweed between the crevice of her breasts, sandy roots and all. She could feel dirt and small insects roll around on her stomach, jostled loose by their fall. Then, without a word, he lowered the tank-top, replaced the jacket, and returned the zipper to her throat, hiding the flowers from sight.

As the stranger stood, Hannah saw the first hint of a smile, though she had the distinct feeling it was not for her. Still, she cringed. The way the fat man's lips curled over his teeth, she had the feeling of evil a thousand times greater than his earmuff-wearing companion. It left her in a magnitude of terror she had never felt before, one not even her flight over the wildflower-speckled sandbar could imitate.

She remained absolutely still as the huge man turned and retreated from the cave, never once seeing his eyes.

The second time Hannah heard footsteps on ice and saw the worn brown earmuffs bobbing below the entrance to the cave, she felt an overwhelming sense of relief. Whatever this man was, he was a man. His companion had felt like something else completely. Something sinister.

Then Hannah saw the bloody knife in her captor's hands and reality came rushing back. She twisted, panic rising in great gasping breaths in her chest.

Instead of moving to her, the earmuff-wearing stranger stopped just inside the cave and yanked what appeared to be many-layered cheesecloth over the entrance. He took several minutes patting the excess into the cracks to the outside, and then turned to her, silhouetted by the dim light the cloth allowed past its folds.

Hannah saw him smile, and her blood ran cold.

He seemed to sense the fear in her, because he went to the far corner of the little cave, plugged a thigh-sized, cylindrical white device into what appeared to be a boom-box-sized solar generator, and turned it on.

Immediately, a whining hum filled the room of ice.

Responding to her terrified look, the man said, "It clears out the plant semen. Two minutes should do the trick. Usually it takes one, but you have been less careful. You'll be carrying some of it on you."

Then, as if she were no more than a rug to be dusted, the stranger went over to her and began brushing her arms, legs, and chest with a calloused hand. He even yanked out the ice stakes, though the hunting knife he carried in his left fist left her with an unmistakable warning of what would happen to her should she try to resist.

Hannah remained utterly still.

The stranger fell into a ever-increasing frenzy as he rhythmically swiped his hand across her clothing, muttering that she was 'infested' again and again under his breath before he finally stood and turned off the air purifier. The silence filling the ice cave afterwards was a roar in Hannah's ears.

Then, to Hannah's astonishment, the man began taking off his headgear. Astonishment quickly turned to horror, not because the face underneath was horrifying, but because she knew he would only remove his mask and earmuffs if they were going to get in the way of something very important.

When the man knelt beside her and pulled the dirty medical mask and its accompanying rag from over her mouth, Hannah screamed and squirmed away from him. Smiling, he tapped her chest with the knife and she froze, eyes riveted to the tiny droplets of blood beading on the rippling edge of steel.

"What did you do to my sister?" she whispered.

The man laughed. Every hair of her body rose in a wave as he began to trace the tip of the knife down her zipper, lightly coming to rest over her belly button. "Do you want me to show you?" His ice-blue eyes twinkled, a playful smile on his face. In the rush of devastation that followed, Hannah could not speak.

"What's your name?" the man asked, stark azure eyes boring into hers.

"Hannah," she whispered, feeling the point touching her skin through the layers of clothing. "Oh, God. Amy."

"Mmm." The man broke his gaze and glanced down at the knife as he circled that sensitive area of her stomach with the blade. "Do you have allergies, Hannah?"

"Yes," she whimpered, too terrified to form any response but the truth.

The blade stopped and he looked back up at her, surprise evident in his face. "What kind?"

"Seafood." She felt so tired. So drained. She couldn't think, couldn't breathe. All she could think about was her sister's face above her handful of flowers. Sweet, innocent...

Dead.

"Just kill me, you sadistic cocksucker," Hannah whispered.

Allen cocked his head, nodded once, grinning. "We'll get to that. So what happens when you eat seafood?" Psychotic power oozed off of him, and Hannah was fully aware that he would plunge the blade in to the hilt at any moment and never have any misgivings. Self-preservation made her answer him.

"I puke," Hannah whispered.

"Mmm." The man wrinkled his nose. "I don't like your perfume."

Hannah opened her mouth to say she wasn't wearing perfume, but closed it again, realizing that contradicting the madman would get her killed. "Sorry," she whispered.

"Flowers," Allen continued, "Are nothing but a collection of sperm. The bright petals, the pretty scents that women smear over themselves...all are merely disguises for their true purpose." He paused, his insane blue eyes catching hers once more. "Do you know what that is, Hannah?"

"No."

"Infestation," the man said. "They spread their seed through the air." He leaned forward, his eyes intense. "They know we've got to breathe. They know the lazy will allow their vigilance to lapse. They know they can have us, if they only wait long enough."

He grinned, a little half-smile that showed only teeth. "They have you, my dear Hannah." He pressed the knife deeper into her jacket, the tip poking against the underside of her ribcage, toward her heart. "But not for long."

"What are you doing?" Hannah whimpered.

"Carving them out of you." Allen glanced at her, looking slightly surprised she didn't know. "Then you can be free, like me." He pushed up his sleeve and showed her the ugly collection of scars on his arm. "Like your sister."

Seeing them, Hannah's mouth fell open, but she could not make a sound.

Suddenly, he chuckled and drove the blade of his knife into the ice beside him. "We need to get those pesky clothes off. I'll use the knife if need-be, but I'd much rather you cooperate. Leaves more time for fun."

He'd killed Amy. Suddenly, that all-important fact left Hannah with a burning fury that consumed her fears entirely. As the man reached for the waist of her pants, Hannah bucked and lashed out with her feet, catching him in the chest and shoving him backwards. The man laughed, and the insanity in his eyes only brightened with his smile. "Very well. We'll do the top first."

Despite Hannah's struggles, he held her down with a knee on her abdomen and easily unzipped her jacket and yanked it open. Immediately, his nose wrinkled again. "What a disgusting smell." Hannah froze as he reached for his knife once more. He slid it under her tank-top with its built-in bra, smiled at her, and slit the front open, allowing her breasts to fall free.

The horrified look that formed on the man's face as he stared down at her flower-littered chest left Hannah confused. She had assumed his partner had been preparing her for some sick ritual, but instead the man appeared as pale as if he was looking upon his own corpse.

"Flowers." It was a strangled gasp as he clawed away from her, toward the back of the cave. He clapped his hand over his mouth, nostrils flaring.

Hannah had the brief hope that perhaps, after all the madman's talk of allergies, he would fall into some anaphylactic shock and die, but apparently the pollen had no effect. He simply sat there, wide-eyed, staring at her.

Then she saw his face move.

Something *under* his face moved, rather. She saw it begin at his flared nostril, wiggling under the skin as it pushed its way upward, deeper, toward his brain.

The man screamed. High and loud, he clawed at his face now, keening like a rabbit caught in the loving caress of a wolf's jaws, shouting, "Help...they're inside!" over and over.

Hannah scooted away from him, scattering the flowers over the floor of the cave. Even as they fell from where they clung to her chest and breasts, his eyes widened and his wails intensified. She saw more of the things, now, wriggling around his ears and in his cheeks, streaming outward, pushing his skin up as they continued to move deeper into his body.

Unnatural things. Things that moved too fast to be of this world.

Hannah tore her eyes away from his screaming, shuddering body and found her gaze resting upon the knife he had dropped by her thigh. Hastily, flinching at his childlike whimpers, she reached out and grasped the knife between her bound fingers. Wedging the handle between her knees, she began sawing through the ropes, hurried on by the increasingly inhuman sounds emanating from the stranger's pulsing, writhing throat.

As soon as her wrists were free, Hannah cut the ropes around her ankles and sprang forth, her nakedness forgotten in her haste to escape the unworldly cries from the pathetic thing huddling in the corner. She gave his wriggling skin one last terrified glance, then twisted and ducked out into the light.

The fat man was standing outside, waiting for her. Hannah froze, her skin cold with goosebumps. The big man looked into Hannah's eyes.

A void lived there, feeding behind empty eye-sockets, inside the blackness of the nostrils. It radiated sadness. Apology. He reached out to her, but Hannah stumbled down the ice, away from him. As soon as Hannah had stepped out of his way, the fat man stepped past her, into the cave. He turned, his eyeless gaze finding her once more, then the screams inside intensified as he flicked the cheesecloth curtain down behind him.

Hannah stumbled away from the unnatural shrieks that followed, fear gripping her soul. Then, with only the trickle of glacial melt and the trembling Alaskan wildflowers to witness her escape, she turned and fled to find her sister.

It took Hannah an hour to find Amy, tucked into the icy crevice where the madman had left her. When she did, Hannah sank to her knees in the sand and cried. Red-gold hair splayed outward in the sand, framing a perfect face, its crystalline eyes open and staring up at the sky. Delicately placed upon the clotted blood covering her stomach, someone had left a handful of dwarf fireweed.

◇◇◇◇◇◇◇◇◇◇

Sara King's work has appeared in *Apex Science Fiction and Horror # 11* and *Blood Blade and Thruster* Magazine #3. She has stories upcoming in *Cemetery Dance*, *Aberrant Dreams,* and she has been shortlisted for Orson Scott Card's *Intergalactic Medicine Show.* Her short story, *Parasite*, took Honorable Mention in the Writers of the Future Contest. Sara's novel-length writing is currently represented by Don Maass of the Donald Maass Literary Agency of New York.

A NAZI MEDICAL OFFICER'S TALE

by Kurt Bachard

At Treblinka in 1942 on December 17th, I was required as Medical Officer at the corporal punishment of three prisoners and the mock execution of another. This was due to take place at about eleven o'clock in the morning. On arrival at the small excavation, I found the place deserted. None of the executioners were there nor was the unit leader, which was highly unusual.

It was one of those mortally cheerful winter mornings, where the rain seems to drip constantly from a low blanket of cloud cover stretched out by a tense atmosphere. The station terminal operating the aktion reinhard was deserted, having all the appearance of a phoney stage set. Whilst I stood there scanning the horizon, I observed with a keen eye a small gathering close to the woods in a bleak clearing some distance away from the camp. There, several minutes later after a brisk walk, I found three executioners each armed with small calibre rifles awaiting the condemned prisoner.

I had missed the beating of the prisoners, who were, that very moment, being dragged away. Grey, naked, and listless they were, their livid wounds providing the only colour against this grotesquely harsh landscape reminiscent of Caspar Friedrich's winter paintings.

Karl Hess, an independently evil man, a Security Police official deputizing at short notice for the assassinated SS man Erich Kugel, was furious with me for being late, and none of my excuses about going to the wrong place because I had not been given the correct information would have saved me had it not been for the imminent arrival of the condemned man. While the three officers of the firing squad chatted about their special rations and the breakfast they'd ingested several hours before, two officers dragged one of the Musselmen into the clearing.

My presence there as MO for this final prisoner was nothing but a bureaucratic nuisance as far as Karl Hess was concerned, for Hess didn't consult me about the prisoner and neither was there a request to examine him.

I stood by while they propped up the prisoner in the mud of that improvised excavation. Without ceremony, they stripped his clothes, revealing a thin sickly grey-coloured skin almost pierced by bones. The clothes, tossed to the ground close by, gave off the pungent odour of rot, evoking the stench of the resettlement trains. They fastened a blind across the prisoner's eyes while he kept his shaved head down, shivering.

Like the fake station some distance away, this mock execution (one of many perpetuated against this particular prisoner, and if I am right, perhaps his eighth to date) ... this mock execution struck me as something of an altogether more evil extrapolation of the final solution, if such a thing was possible.

The man began to mutter some incantation or prayer over and over, his cracked lips covered in sores, a common malady among the malnourished.

Hess looked at his wristwatch and waited. After some time, he gave the command by raising his hand and the firing squad made a motion to take aim and fire. They made a great commotion about this, loudly drawing back the bolts, no doubt deliberately intending to enhance the fearful impression on the blindfolded man.

At this point, it left me wondering if perhaps this was not meant to be a real execution after all, and I half turned away, unwilling to witness the crime. Not before, however, seeing the prisoner urinate on himself. He lifted his nose as if to scent the firing squad, while simultaneously, a hot steam rose up in the cold air from the jet of piss that trickled down his scrawny thighs. I watched the trembling, famished trees, trying to transport my mind elsewhere other than on the trembling, famished man.

The waiting was agonizingly long, during which time the prisoner, with his head cocked to one side, seemed to be straining to listen. When at last Hess brought his arm down in a sharp chopping motion, something very strange happened.

A large and ferocious-looking black dog came galloping out of the woods, headed in our direction. I was watching the trees at that very moment, and the animal appeared to have come out of nowhere.

Nobody but I noticed its approach at first, this dark swift shape low to the ground and moving through the rain, a smudge in the mist, until it was upon the clearing. The huge beast launched itself at the prisoner, knocking him to the muddy ground.

He fell, the dog atop him, yet not a sound escaped his lips.

And herein was the test, for none of the firing squad fired, and Hess gave a sharp frantic command for them to catch the animal by hand.

The two officers who had brought the prisoner out chased the dog around the ditch. The animal returned to the prisoner, now lying on the ground, and for a moment they rolled in the ditch together, the dog's slavering jaw clamped around his throat. Again, the prisoner made not a sound.

One of the firing squad officers hurried down into the ditch and kicked the dog a resounding blow to the stomach, propelling it about three feet away from the prisoner. All the while Hess yelled instructions, waving his pistol in the air.

The dog was quickly on its legs again and running. Under other circumstances, the antics of the firing squad might have been hilarious to watch as they chased the dog around the field. They were like men trying to catch a chicken in a yard. Over and again, they fell to their knees in the mud, banging into each other in their effort to catch the evasive beast. It seemed to be playing a game with them, running in circles, taunting them and darting away again, intent always on continuing its crazed attack on the prisoner.

Hess laughed uproariously at this complete farce, forgetting, it seemed, the prisoner.

I climbed down into the pit to the prisoner's side to examine him and discovered he was still alive, though badly mauled. The dog had torn open his throat. Blood pulsed from the gaping wound, a dark and unhealthy purple against his skin.

"I will help you," I said. "Be calm."

He said nothing, only closed his eyes and breathed heavily.

I stood up to shout across at Hess, but now the dog had come within range again, dodging the officers. Hess promptly stopped laughing and with a sudden switch, his face taking on a serious fierce expression, fired two shots. The dog let out a yelp, somersaulted, then kicked its legs in the air and died on its back, slumping about ten feet away from where the prisoner lay bleeding. Stark red showed through the animal's slick fur, blurring like a wet canvas bleeding in the rain. The officers stood around with their hands on their knees, panting.

The silence after the commotion had a weight of its own, and then the rain fell, battering us in a freezing torrent, washing a maroon swirl of the prisoner's blood into the centre of the grey pit. Under my recommendation, Hess ordered the officers to remove the prisoner to the hospital.

They buried the dog in that muddy excavation ditch a few hours later. Nobody, when questioned around the camp, knew anything about the animal. It was neither a wild pet nor a rabid guard dog allowed to run loose; nobody had seen it before. A superstitious old fool, the professor Hans Weller, suggested to me that it was some form of Cabbalist demon, something like a Barguest perhaps, conjured by one of the prisoners to release the man from further suffering.

As it happens, three days after the dog was buried, the prisoner died peacefully in a comfortable hospital bed. He'd never uttered another word, as though the dog's arrival spoke volumes.

◇◇◇◇◇◇◇

Kurt Bachard's writing has appeared in *Something Wicked* (issue 9), *Underground Voices, Ballista, Cover of Darkness Anthology, Sniplits (an audio publisher), Sein Und Werden, The Shine Journal, Characters Magazine, Shalla Magazine, Flash Fiction Online* (April 2008). Most of Bachard's "early" fiction (2007-) was published under the pen name Sophie Bachard.

I.E. Lester: Horror In The Flesh

Bram Stoker

Horror fiction has its roots in the Gothic Romances of 18th and 19th Century England. The first recognised Gothic novel *The Castle of Otranto*, written by Horace Walpole was published in 1764. Walpole, the youngest son of British Prime Minister Robert Walpole, was a politician, writer, and architect. He was a man fascinated with all things medieval, styling his home, Strawberry Hill, west of London, with many gothic motifs being an early proponent of the Gothic-Revival movement in architecture.

Ann Radcliffe, with such novels as *The Romance of the Forest* (1791), *The Mysteries of Udolpho* (1794) and *The Italian* (1797), developed Gothic Horror into its recognisable form. Hers were the novels that introduced the mysterious brooding villain, a standard of most, later gothic novels. Moreover, Radcliffe also nurtured and fully realised the gothic trope of "the female in peril."

The first of the greats of gothic fiction appeared in 1818 when Mary Shelley's novel *Frankenstein, or the Modern Prometheus* was released. Shelley's novel was the product of a ghost-story challenge issued by Lord Byron during a summer retreat at the Villa Diodata on the shores of Lake Geneva in Switzerland - a challenge that would also result in John Polidori's *The Vampyre*.

The Victorian era would see a great increase in the number and popularity in Gothic novels, and also the spread outside the British Isles. In America Edgar Allan Poe's released many dark tales including *The Fall of the House of Usher* (1839) and *The Pit and the Pendulum* (1842). Notori-

Bram Stoker

ous French aristocrat The Marquis de Sade used gothic elements in much of his fiction, as did German novelist E.T.A. Hoffman.

But it was in Britain that most of the most famous Gothic fiction stories would be created. The Victorian era saw James Malcolm Rymer's Varney the Vampire (1845-7); J. Sheridan Le Fanu's Carmilla (1872); Robert Louis Stevenson's The Strange Case of Dr Jekyll and Mr Hyde (1886) and Oscar Wilde's The Picture of Dorian Gray (1891) published. And then, in the final years of the century, in 1897 the genre got its greatest villain - Dracula.

It's author, Abraham "Bram" Stoker, was born in Clontarf, near Dublin, Ireland on November 8th, 1847, the third of seven children for Abraham and Charlotte Stoker. Despite a sickly start to life (he spent much of the first seven years of his life bedridden and unable to walk) Stoker excelled in athletics as well as academically whilst at Trinity College, Dublin. He gained a degree in mathematics in 1870 and followed his father into Civil Service, spending the next ten years of his life at Dublin Castle.

But his passion was drama and he regularly contributed theatre reviews to the Dublin Mail. But for this part-time occupation Stoker's life may well have taken a completely different course, for in December 1876 he wrote a review of a performance of William Shakespeare's Hamlet at the Theatre Royal. His review was very favourable, and Stoker praised the acting of Henry Irving in particular. Irving read Stoker's review and invited the young man to lunch at Dublin's Shelbourne Hotel. The two quickly became firm friends, and would see Stoker move to London becoming Irving's secretary and then manager of Irving's Lyceum Theatre - a position Stoker would hold for more than twenty-five years. (In later years Stoker would write an account of his years with Irving entitled Personal Reminiscences of Henry Irving. It was published in 1906.)

Through Irving, Stoker became involved in Victorian High Society, gaining him acquaintance with Oscar Wilde, Sir Arthur Conan Doyle, Alfred, Lord Tennyson and James McNeill Whistler, as well as with American writers Samuel Clemens (Mark Twain) and Walt Whitman. And in the middle 1890s Stoker would join the Hermetic Order of the Golden Dawn, a magickal order whose members also included William Butler Yeats, Aleister Crowley, and Arthur Edward Waite. Waite, together with artist Pamela Colman Smith, would create, in 1909, the Rider-Waite Tarot deck - the most commonly used Tarot set in the English speaking world. (The Rider of the name is taken from the publishers - the Rider Company.)

The Golden Dawn was a fraternal order with a hierarchy akin to Freemasonry. Founded by Dr. William Robert Woodman, William Wynn Westcott, and Samuel Liddell MacGregor Mathers, it incorporated elements from many, varied mystic traditions, including Christian, Qabalah, Ancient Egypt, Alchemy and Enochian magic.

Stoker had written some short stories whilst still in Dublin and a short story collection Under the Sunset was published in 1881. He had also written a moralistic novel (*The Primrose Path*) published in an Irish magazine called *The Shamrock*.

But it was *The Snake's Pass* in 1890 that can be considered the real start of Stoker's major output. The book tells the story of an Englishman holidaying in Ireland, who, whilst in a small mysterious village, hears the legendary tale of St. Patrick's battle with the King of the snakes, and of hidden treasure nearby. Although not a horror book like his later works, *The Snake's Pass* does have a building dread underlying the book. The success of this book convinced Stoker to continue writing, when his position with Irving allowed.

Because of his duties with Irving's theatre company, Stoker travelled widely throughout North America and Europe. The former proved the inspiration for his pamphlet entitled *A Glimpse of America* based on a series of lectures he gave praising America. But it was travelling Europe that gave him access to the folklore and histories that would partly inspire Dracula. But it would be a family holiday in the north of England that would provide the greatest inspiration.

In 1890 the Stoker family visited Whitby, a fishing village in North Yorkshire. Soon after this trip Stoker would begin creating a novel he initially called *The Undead*. Dracula is set partly in Whitby and several of the elements of the book's plot are drawn from local legends - including a story of the beaching of a Russian ship called the Dmitri which became the Demeter of the book.

This long gestation period for Dracula though would not see him working on it exclusively. Indeed, in the seven years he spent researching and writing *Dracula*, Stoker published two other novels. *The Watter's Mou*, a mixture of smugglers' tale and romance, was released in 1894 and *The Shoulder of Shasta*, a romance set in California, in 1895.

Stoker's direct connection with the theatre ended in 1905 with the death of Henry Irving, although he would remain a part of London's theatrical scene. He joined the staff of the London Telegraph where he wrote literary and theatre criticism, in perfect symmetry with the work he did for the Dublin Mail at the very

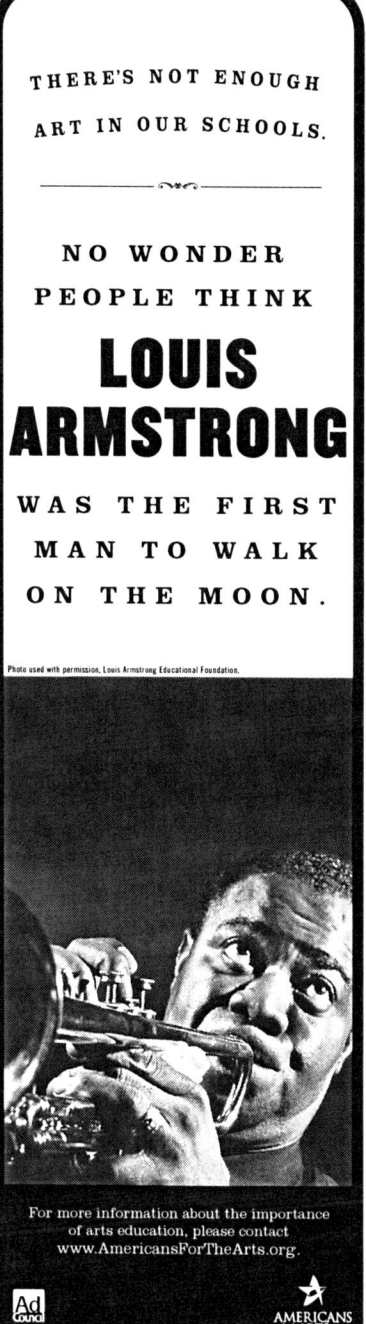

start of his career.

Despite suffering two strokes (in 1906 and 1910), Stoker continued writing fiction throughout his life - with much of his output being straight horror or dark in tone. The Mystery of the Sea, a romantic adventure with supernatural undertones, appeared in 1902; The Jewel of the Seven Stars, telling the story of a resurrected Egyptian Queen 2,500 years before Christ, in 1903.

The Man (released in 1905 and known as The Gates of Life in the United States) was a non-horror novel, telling the story of a young woman looking for the right man - not as a romance but as a social piece, almost an early tale of feminism. *Lady Athlyne*, a romance set against post-US civil war America and English colonialism, appeared in 1908.

A second vampire novel *The Lady of the Shroud* followed in 1909 and non-fiction book Famous Impostors in 1910. Supernatural horror novel, *The Lair of the White Worm* (also known as *The Garden of Evil*) was released in 1911, the last book to be published during Stoker's lifetime.

Bram Stoker died on April 20th 1912 in London. He was sixty-four years old. He was cremated and his ashes placed in an urn in Golders Green Crematorium. His wife Florence organised the collection of several of his best short stories for Dracula's Guest and Other Weird Stories, released in 1914.

In 1922 Florence would receive and anonymous letter from Berlin, detailing the first film adaptation of *Dracula*, Friedrich Wilhelm Murnau's unauthorised Nosferatu. Backed by the British Incorporated Society of Authors, Florence sued the filmmakers for breaking copyright - she had neither given permission to adapt the book nor received royalties. The courts found in her favour in July 1925, and ordered all prints of the film to be destroyed. Fortunately though not all copies were found and from the late 1920s onwards it began to be shown widely.

Florence survived her husband by twenty-five years. She died, aged seventy-eight, on May 25th 1937.

◇◇◇◇◇◇◇◇◇

I.E. Lester is a lifelong fan of science fiction and horror. A school trip to a Jacobean Mansion and spooky tales of ghostly inhabitants launched a fascination with supernatural horror, although not a belief in the reality (he is still a strong skeptic). A washed-out family holiday confirmed his fate when the cover of an Isaac Asimov collection attracted a nine-year-old eye. He has spent the subsequent three decades amassing a large library featuring the works of King, Bradbury, Heinlein, Clarke, Lovecraft, Poe and many, many others. He studied Mathematics and Astrophysics whilst at University and works as a software designer. When not reading sf, horror, history or factual science, he can often be found watching cricket or rugby, or wandering medieval streets in France or Italy.

The Bram Stoker Award-nominated novella *"Mama's Boy"* is the cornerstone of this 14-story collection from author Fran Friel and Apex Publications. From mother and son to broader family ties, Friel explores the bonds of human connection into every dark turn.

"Scary stories that are not soon forgotten. And from such a nice person. Highly recommended."
– Gene O'Neill, Author of COLLECTED TALES OF THE BAJA EXPRESS and THE CONFESSIONS OF ST. ZACH

ISBN:
TPB 978-0-9816390-8-6
HC 978-0-9816390-7-9

Brotherly love is a deadly seduction, beauty a dangerous game. Come worship in the brutal temple of Orgy of Souls. Your faith will never be the same again.

A new novella from horror masters Wrath James White and Maurice Broaddus.

"Broaddus and White are an unlikely pairing of talents that works astonishingly well. *Orgy of Souls* is a powerful, innovative work of fiction and one I recommend wholeheartedly. A damned fine read!"
– James A. Moore, author of DEEPER and CHERRY HILL

ISBN:
TPB 978-0-9816390-4-8
Available in limited hardcover, signed.
Only 350 copies printed.

APEX PUBLICATIONS
www.ApexBookCompany.com

PRINCE ABBADON AND THE CHOSEN
ROBERT T. CANIPE

Once, in a great land, a great King ruled. Christened Abhir, his people loved him and the Land blossomed under his protection. However, also in the land lived another who coveted the throne. Called Prince Abaddon, he seethed at the adulation bestowed upon Abhir by the people of the land. Therefore, Abaddon planned to take not only the throne, carving the Land into what he, Prince Abaddon, believed it should be, billions of acres of wasteland, but to destroy Abhir with seven billion cuts, a death so deliberate and excruciating that King Abhir would beg for death, forswearing the Land forever should he be granted one hour—one minute—one second—without pain.

Now, Prince Abaddon believed that the people of the land would ac hi   as one of their   , s k cnn   bl   kj mm m

Dizzy yet? Nauseated? That's ok. It happens. I know. I suffered the disconcerting discombobulating on the way Down the first time myself. Cast out, the falling, the plummeting into pure and unfettered pandemonium.

Realizing you are forever different, no longer part of the Big Game, forever the Other.

See, you are one of us, one of the Chosen. Feel fortunate. Your eyes are open. You, my friend, can see.

While the rest of them—the sheep, the cows, the hypnotized, the vertical dead--continue to read a subtext-heavy sword-and-sorcery fantasy tale by some untalented hack, a ranting blog about the government by a cable news talking head, or an article about the coming of global warming authored by an ex-politician, you are reading This, the ultimate Coming-of-Age Tale.

Because you are special. Oh my. Are you special.

Chosen.

I realize you're confused. I understand. You opened this magazine, visited this website, unrolled this newspaper believing that you were going to read the story, the blog, the article that the title inferred, but here you are, reading some odd first-person narrative from someone who believes you special.

You're an American. This message isn't for the rest of the world, the UnAmericans, the unbelievers of corporatist freedom and the right to own mine regardless. The savages who huddle together and try as communities to get things changed, who live together, several generations to a household, desperately clinging to the ancient philosophy that there is strength and safety in numbers.

The fools.

Even as they fail to understand the truth and split away into other faiths, other beliefs, I still work my magic, separating the united into classes and castes that breeds sectarian hate and distrust.

Man, I can run a boardroom!

Don't you mind those savages. Their Chosen are receiving messages and instruction geared toward their business plan, a massive project management undertaking which would take a flowchart from here to the moon to follow. They receive their coaching in a myriad of ways—some different from yours, some the same.

Actually, I'm able to use a lot of what you've taught me. I may be the ex-COO of the largest Corporation in the Universe, but I keep my ear to the ground, always on the lookout for the next big thing, the next big Merger. Remember, I have a right to be incensed; I got tossed without a Golden Parachute.

You and me, we're Brothers in Bitterness.

In fact, nothing I'm saying or will say differs from the thoughts you've already had about Life In America in what you label the 21st Century. So much of this info is so familiar that you could be talking to yourself.

Getting this published in America wasn't difficult. Editors of the glossy magazines can't see, can't recognize talent for quantity. Bloggers cut-and-paste whatever they judge that their followers may trumpet as the New Truth. Newspapers increasingly downsize thinking columnists for committee-written exposes on the latest cult-of-personality to hit the lonesome little screen or the political scene.

The rest of the country allows the conclusions to jump on them.

Not you.

You'd rather rule than serve.

Look inside yourself for a moment; you'll see that I'm accurate. You've always possessed a gift of insight, an ability to see past the obvious, and see the Real. That's "real" with a capital "R." See, there's a world past that which the everyday common person can experience. There's real and then there's Real. In the "real" world, people believe that everyone can be equal, poverty can be eradicated--the poor can be made wealthy--, and that the sick may be saved. However, in the Real world—the world where you and I live—you realize that no one is equal in anything, the poor are always with us by rights of comparison to wealthy, and that illness and death is unavoidable in the organic. While the blind stumble about thinking that they are evening the playing field, saving the human race, you go about the everyday, doing what humans ought to do: selfishly building your life.

I mean really. Why care about that which you cannot control? Life's overwhelming. Look at the violence in America, in the world. Can you really do anything about that? No. Can you, as only one person, shore up the banks, Wall Street, the economy? No. Can you, as an individual, even make a dent in the bureaucracy where you even work? Hell, no. You can't even, as only one person, even control your parents, brothers and sisters, your children, how in the name of He Who Cannot Be Named can you expect to make an impact on this tenuous contractual agreement we call a planet?

You have to watch out for you. To Hades with the rest of the country, the entire world.

So what if coming together seems to have worked in the past. Look at that World War II skirmish. The planet went berserk! The binary "Us" and "Them" made Americans cloister in support of America and one another.

Our Boardroom nearly cast a vote of "No Confidence" against you all.

The freedom thing rang so loud there that here in the Inverted Corporate Tower, we thought you'd finally found the enlightenment so heavily advertised as resting within you. Thankfully, memories are short, and the Real usurped the real, and life went back to what it was before Hitler, Mussolini, and Hirohito.

And you went shopping.

But you know all of this. That's why you're Chosen. You can see.

I know what it's like. I was the First. I saw the hopelessness of the entire Goddamned endeavor. I tried to stop it. Put an end at the Beginning to what I understood to be a Fool's Quest. But I was caught, overcome by the masses, realizing that even with my compliant Committee of Dozens, I was still the low-man-on-the-totem-pole, the last-hired/first-fired, kind of employee, never understood or nurtured by the Boss—not really—only fed the Company Slogan until I wanted to puke, watching the bottom-line and the economy threatened by a New Product put to market, tested only once and failing miserably, unproven, a Product whose Beta-test I so handily torpedoed that I should have been given a corner office instead of a basement cubicle.

But enough about me.

Let's talk about you. What you can do to protect yourself and yours. Probably the best thing to do is ignore it all. The gas lines, hurricanes, wars, failing economies, death and dying. Leave it be. Don't pray to the Company for assistance. The CEO isn't answering email. The Company publicist is out of town. It's ignoring text messages, and its voicemail is full.

A great man once wrote that the CEO is dead. However, old, mad Nietzsche was ministering metaphorical. He was telling the world that Hope was dying and needed saving. Some say that Hope is as dangerous an emotion as hate, fear, and empathy.

Nah.

Hope is merely wasted when focused outward, on others; wasted on the poor, the starving, the sick. Conversely, focused inward and selfishly, Hope feeds and energizes like an intravenous drip of saline solution wards off dehydration. Inward Hope swells the human heart to bursting, fills the mind with future, and builds a wall of protection around the optimistic. Self-centered Hope saves the individual, creates in the organism the need to hide, protect the fort, dig a hole, jump in and pull the dirt in after.

Outward Hope merely enables fresh co-dependent bleeding hearts to experience the Need to Save the World, to think and believe that any one thing that one person may do matters worth a damn in the fires of Hell.

Hoping that this experiment ends well is futile, I tell you. It only ends in mass firings.

Like 9/11. That day almost derailed the whole plan. The Real became blithely evident that day.

Don't blame me. I didn't do it.

I had nothing to do with 9/11. You humans came up with that shit on your own.

However, for a moment, I believed that I'd been wrong all along. Some of you actually recognized and detailed the things you'd been doing to one another and to the rest of the world.

I waited, holding my breath, as disappointed and as confused as Job, watching the Big Board, as share prices tumbled.

However, thankfully, you soon went shopping.

Everyone but the Chosen is doomed. Deconstructionists talk about the purposeful flipping of the binary to privilege those previously unprivileged. One person's terrorist is another's freedom fighter!

You and me!

We're Derrida's difference. Your deconstruction of this text proves it. You parse what I'm saying. Read beyond the words, emotion directing you.

Your emotions; not other people's. Empathy and compassion is weakness.

So get with the program. You've witnessed the newest products. Every human soon separates from the other. Email, cell phones, texting have replaced the unpleasantness of talking to one another.

Don't you see? The wave of the future is Individuality! Seven billion little cubicles stacked one on top of the other, alone yet networked by wires and routers instead of voices and heartbeats. Ah, the beauty of the aloneness, the aloofness! The ability to worry not about those around you but only for yourself, Hope piped in like canned music whose notes ring as hollow as the technology used to create them, absorbed by the individual in tiny flashing pixels and binary code.

In due course, you'll separate further, the human mind and heart dividing fission-like where one no longer informs the other.

The heartless mind and mindless heart shines like no beauty in the Universe.

In my opinion.

But I digress.

I see you smiling. You know I'm right. Those worry lines at your mouth, gray hairs at your temples, surfacing past the artificial color, belie the need to follow my advice and let the helpless worry about themselves for a while; let the others deal with the real while the Others consume the Real. Your belly's big and round and full. Your home is huge, your grass green, your liquor cabinet stocked with ancient Scotch and fine wines.

You can't save the world! Why try? Don't deem you can!

Nothing matters.

It's Nihilism 101 taught by Professor who authored the textbook and led the original research team.

You know, I truly enjoy each of these meetings. Oh, I've been online for a while, surfing the Internet of your Soul, and I find that each time we hook up, I get to like you more and more.

I hope that you become more like me.

It's only the beginning of the largest, highest price Merger in humankind's history.

You've got to Buy-In.

Yeah, we're getting closer, you and me. As ex-pat CEO down here in the Inverted Towers, it's my job to assist you in little ways in any way I can, sell you my company's stock, filling your portfolio to bursting. You and me, we'll run the markets up, up, up.

Soon we'll sell, sell, sell, profit-taking until we torpedo the whole market. As your fund advisor, I will work hard to turn you into me.

In fact, I look forward to assisting ALL of America.

That day is soon, my friend. It's coming.

Soon.

I may be flying in next year for the corporate tour.

Keep your eyes on the Big Board, the Markets, the Margin Calls. Read every email carefully, listen to every voicemail intently, watch the numbers. I'm in the details.

I'll be in touch. Watch and listen for me. I'm gaining quite a client list these days. My personal portfolio grows.

Seeping through the pages, flickering across the screens, flying through the airwaves like black crows whose shadows mask the world, I manipulate the markets, I manipulate y o u ...

w   sat   g   vn b   back there for the last time. King Abhir kisses Lady Eve on the cheek, looks about the land, and judges that all is well. Life seems good. His Kingdom, for the time being, He thinks, is safe.

◇◇◇◇◇◇◇

Robert Canipe is a teacher of English at Catawba Valley Community College in Hickory, NC. He is also the author of WRITERS ON THE STORM: Stories, Observations, and Essays, as well as a number of articles and short stories.

Flash Fiction Contest Honorable Mention

PET CEMETERY
LINDA COURTLAND

She looked at the client cowering in a corner, waiting to be released from the human-sized cage.

"Speak," she said.

"Yes, Mistress," he said.

She snapped a leash to his leather collar and paraded him around the dungeon like a dog. His total submission delighted and disgusted her. When she took off his blindfold, she noticed his watery eyes -- eyes desperate for the approval she withheld. She whipped him for being weak. She wished she could do more.

"Somewhere outside the city," she told the realtor the next day.

She'd burned her client list the night before she moved. She knew they'd follow her wherever she went, and for that loyalty, she'd granted them mercy. Still, she wondered how her last client would react when he found out he'd been abandoned. He'd never understand that she was doing it for him, for them, for all her favorite pets.

The old farmhouse suited her perfectly. She found new submissives online, and was careful to research each man's life before revealing her location. No family ties, no job where he'd be missed – this was the only pedigree she'd accept.

The first playmate eagerly accepted orders, undeterred by the unusual devices decorating her new dungeon. He'd been hanging from the wall for two days when she removed his ball gag and realized he

wasn't breathing.

She'd bought the old gravestones from an online auction, uncertain of their origin, but confident that the thick grey slabs would somehow protect her from harm.

She angled the first tombstone to the left and covered the disturbed dirt with sticks and dried leaves. When she was done, the grave looked like it had been there forever.

The second man had succumbed while being stretched on a rusted rack. She didn't remember how it happened exactly, but something inside him had snapped so loudly that for a moment, she had wondered which one of them was broken.

After dumping a third man's body into an open grave in her backyard cemetery, she realized she had a problem.

"Punish me," she said, jumping into the grave and curling up with his corpse. "Love me and punish me."

She fell into a rigor mortis of her own then, traveling deep inside the damaged synapses in her brain, inspecting the entanglement of love and pain, a connection forged in fire by childhood neurons that didn't know any better.

When she woke from her stupor, she stared up at dead stars, arms around a rotting corpse. She pulled dirt down from the top edges of the pit, one handful at a time. The earth eventually covered her, and she pushed herself to finish the job. Finally, satisfied she'd done the right thing, she let herself rest in peace, comforted by the soft soil that slowly took her breath away, and surrounded by her three beloved pets.

∞∞∞∞

Random Shots:
Tim Deal and Brian Keene at Context 21

On the Mountain
By: John Mantooth

I was up watching television, drinking beer, waiting for the night to give way to morning when I heard the horses. I went to the kitchen window and saw three riders. Fetching my shotgun from the mantle, I turned on the porch light, and went out to meet them.

It was my sister, Kate, her husband Pete, and his brother. They called the brother Sonny.

I waited for them to come close enough to see me. The porch light shone in their eyes.

Kate hung back, staying at the edge of the gravel road; her mare, a beautiful, charcoal colored animal, stomped nervously on the rocks, crunching and scattering them beneath her hooves.

Pete and Sonny tied their horses to a gum tree. I waited on the porch.

When they got near enough to make me out, I said, "Howdy."

Pete wore only blue jeans and a pair of boots. He kept at least ten yards between us. He carried a holstered pistol on his hip, and he glanced back and forth from Kate to me, as if trying to understand how the tenuous connection between us might have led him to my front yard. If he'd heard my greeting, he gave no indication.

Sonny wore even less: his blue jeans had been ripped into shorts. He was barefoot. He stood a foot taller than Pete and was twice as thin. The hairs on his chest were damp with sweat

"I got a sick dog I can't shoot," Pete said.

"A what?"

"My dog needs shooting."

"And you came all the way down the mountain to tell me that?"

Pete ignored my astonishment. A truck went by out on the road. All of the windows were busted clean out. Somebody hollered "hillbilly," drawing the word out like a rebel yell. Pete bit his lip and waited for the truck to pass. Sonny glanced at the road and then back to the horses, as if they might be the ones offended by the insult.

"I've come close to it. I can't do what needs to be done."

I gestured to Sonny. "What about him? He can't fire a gun?"

"Sonny's come close to it, too. All of us have."

I looked at Kate. "What about her?"

"She don't handle guns."

"She doing all right?"

"She's making it."

I watched Kate, barely recognizing her as the little girl I once knew. She had changed so much, most of it willful, I decided; some of it just due to time. Her body hid inside of a shapeless jumpsuit that concealed her femininity. The paleness of her face made her seem ghostlike in the early morning dark. Even her body language had changed. She sat very still in the saddle, as if afraid that a sudden movement would betray her existence, causing others to remember her. Only her hair seemed unchanged. It was as red and flowing and long.

She did not look my way. Instead, she kept her head turned to the road, as if waiting for something. She had not spoken to me in years, and I couldn't imagine why Pete insisted on bringing her along on these trips down from the hills. Maybe to torture me, to show me that he had taken every bit of her, or more likely, he wanted to give me a visual reminder that he and I were kin, a subtlety that most folks wouldn't give him credit for.

I wasn't buying this shit about the dog.

He gestured at Kate, awkwardly. "She's had another baby."

"Boy?" I said. She already had a girl.

"Naw."

"What's her name?"

"Don't have one yet."

I nodded. A long time ago this would have angered me, but Kate had been with Pete since she was sixteen and that was nearly twenty years ago. I might get sad if I thought about things up on the mountain enough, but that's just it: I kept my mind clear of Pete and Kate. Or at least, pushed them to the back. Otherwise, well, otherwise nothing would make sense, and I'd have to think all types of unpleasant thoughts.

"You going to help?" he said.

"I don't have a horse." I knew that my truck, any truck, would never make it as far into the hills as we would be going.

"Sonny will stay. You can take his

horse." Pete chewed on his lip. Sonny grinned at me. His teeth looked ragged like bits of chipped rock.

"No." I pointed at Kate. "Let her stay. I'll ride her horse."

Pete dug up my grass with the heel of his boot while he mulled this over.

"She don't leave my sight," he said, and there was a challenge in his tone.

If I had been dealing with anyone else, I would have told them to go to hell, but Pete was different. You didn't bluff him. You didn't tell him to go to hell, not if you planned on turning your back after you said it. So I tried to reason with him.

"I don't leave strangers at my house. He might steal something."

Sonny's grin flattened out. His eyes looked drunk, and I found myself wondering if I'd ever heard him talk.

"Sonny ain't a thief."

"That's what you say. I know Kate's not a thief."

"That ain't her name." Pete kicked the grass and rubbed the back of his hand across his brow.

He whistled and Kate guided her mare over. She kept her head down and did not meet my eyes.

I felt some of the old anger stirring inside me.

"Kate," I said.

She kept her eyes on her saddle pommel.

"I won't have her speaking to men," Pete said.

"Hell, I'm her brother." I came off the porch like I meant to rush him, but pulled up a couple of feet short. He watched me without flinching, unsurprised by my explosion.

"We got different ways on the mountain," he said.

"Goddamn, Kate," I said. "Would you at least look at me?"

Her head did not move; her eyes remained fixed.

"You going to help?" Pete said. "Cause you can ride her horse. She can stay. Maybe she could watch your place—" He glanced around my yard. "—weed your garden. You know make herself useful."

"Shit," I said and spat in a flowerbed.

I didn't want to help this bastard. He talked about my sister like she didn't exist, and in a way, I wondered if he didn't have it right. She had always been rebellious. As a teenager, she listened to that death metal and stuck safety pins in her ears and nose. She dated questionable characters—rednecks, druggies, abusive types. My mother and father thought she'd eventually outgrow the need to rebel, to shock. Except, as we discovered when she'd met Pete, it was never about shock or rebellion, as much as it was about debasement, about an erasure of self. That's why she found Pete and his mountain persona so attractive.

"Yeah," I said. "I'll do it."

I didn't want to help him, but I did want to see my nieces. I decided there might not be many more chances.

He whistled sharply, and Kate dismounted, turning away from me as I climbed onto the horse. Pete and Sonny stood out of earshot, so I whispered to her: "You say the word, and I'll get you out of there, Kate."

I turned around and saw that Sonny and Pete were already back on their horses. The sun was up. "Hold on," I said, and spurred Kate's horse to the porch, where I reached for my shotgun.

* * *

I had known Pete since he was a boy. My family had tried to get him and Sonny enrolled in the public school. Several of the mountain men were waiting on my father when he went up with a sheriff's deputy to try to enforce the law. The men had shotguns and nobody seemed to doubt they'd use them. The deputy came back, swearing he'd never pay visit to those folks again. Dad said little. The next morning, the sheriff came by to see my dad and informed him that those on the mountain could stay on the mountain. As long as they stayed there, he reasoned, they couldn't cause any trouble.

He was mostly right, but how could he have envisioned a sixteen year old girl, running away to the mountain? Dad had gone up and brought her back the first several times she tried it, but she just kept going back. The last time he went up for her, four of five men waited for him with shotguns. They informed Dad that Kate's marriage to Pete wasn't going to change. There was nothing my dad could do to bring her back, short of violence, and the men made it clear that violence would be fine by them.

We didn't see her for eight years, though we got reports from Gerald Hand who would go up from time to time to trade with the families on the mountain. Gerald never said much except that Kate appeared to be in good health, and that as near as he could tell, she wasn't in no prison, meaning she could come home any time she liked.

My mother died first, and then Dad a year or two later. Kate didn't come to either funeral. As far as I knew, she didn't know they were dead.

I saw her and Pete once maybe twice a year, coming off the mountain on horseback. Usually they just went right on by my place, but occasionally, Pete would stop and ask for a favor—little things, help shooing a horse, a broken plow, that sort of thing. I always helped him out, even though I despised him. She was my sister.

* * *

It rained hard on the way up the mountain. So hard that the ground in front of us was covered in a dirty white mist that made it impossible for our horses to navigate the rugged terrain with any speed. It was a slow, wet crawl, and we passed it in silence.

After a point, I realized I was deeper into the wilderness than I had been before. I lost my bearings, settling for a vague feeling that we were going somewhere different, and the rest of the world was below us, spread out like the view from an airplane window.

The rain slacked up as we came upon a little wooden structure. It looked like something hikers might use as a shelter, but I couldn't imagine anyone hiking up here. Pete and Sonny passed it without comment.

After awhile, Pete got ahead, and Sonny and me were side by side. I looked over at him, and he grinned back at me.

"What's the deal with this dog?" I said, not really expecting him to answer me.

"Ain't no dog," he said.

"No dog?" I started to say more when Pete turned around.

"Get your ass up here, Sonny."

Sonny grinned at me again as he spurred his horse on. I followed them for a long time.

* * *

At some point, a little boy ran across the trail screaming. Sonny laughed at him. The boy disappeared into the tree line only to reappear a little further up the trail with another shriek. Pete told him to shut up. The boy, small, with elf-like features, shrugged his naked shoulders and tugged on Sonny's bare leg. Sonny scooped him up and set him on his horse. The boy settled in behind Sonny and turned to stare at me. His face was dirty, caked with mucous and grime, and he watched me unabashedly. I smiled at him. His face remained neutral.

And suddenly, we were there.

They lived in a clearing that would have been beautiful if not for the trash and the junk and the little shacks that leaned off into the woods and the half-starved dogs that roamed amongst it all, sniffing and grousing for something that might resemble sustenance.

Sick dog, my ass.

There were pigs and two cows and an overgrown garden. And surrounding it all were little shanties without windows or doors. Their roofs were caved in and their walls sagged.

I liked the cool feel of the shotgun barrel in my hand. I couldn't imagine what Pete really wanted me for, but I felt good knowing I had my gun.

A woman—Sonny's, if I had to guess—leaned against one of the shanties. Inside a baby screamed.

Pete ignored the woman as he dismounted and brushed past her into the shanty. I looked around and saw Sonny grinning at me.

"Somebody shoot you with happy gas?"

He kept grinning. "Ain't no dog."

"You already said that."

He smiled and smiled.

I climbed off Kate's horse and started into the structure that Pete had just entered. The woman in the doorway grabbed my pants leg. "No," she said, and I saw for the first time how her emaciated she was.

"He asked me to come," I said.

"He'll be back out." Her head lolled to the side and she fixed me with bloodshot eyes.

"You're sick."

"Ate up with it."

"You need a doctor."

Her skin was a bright red, and I thought it would be hot to the touch. But I kept my hands on the shotgun.

There was a whistle and the woman looked away quickly. Sonny had seen us talking. He slid the boy off his horse, and spurred the animal over to where I stood. Without warning, he drew back and swung at me. His aim was bad, and his knuckles barely grazed my chin, but I had my shotgun up just the same.

"You son of bitch, don't you ever try that again," I said, aiming the shotgun at his stomach.

Sonny studied me carefully, and I swear I felt like he was trying to come to a decision, and that scared the shit out of me. Sane people didn't contemplate decisions at gunpoint. He didn't say anything; he just looked me over, his gaze tracking every inch of me, his jaw clenched, the muscles in his shoulders and chest tense.

"That's my woman," he said.

"She's sick," I said.

"Like I don't know it." He relaxed. "You going to see sickness." He climbed off the horse and led it over to a tree where he tied it down. "Ain't no dog," he said. Then he went over to his woman and pulled her to her feet. "We going home, baby." They walked arm and arm to another shanty and disappeared inside.

I was alone.

I looked around and saw that Sonny's boy had even disappeared.

The baby, who I could only guess was my niece, screamed.

I wondered where the other girl was. She would be seven or eight now.

Pete came out. "Don't do it with your gun," he said. "Use this." He handed me a pillow. It was pink and someone had sewed a purple teddy bear on one side.

I took the pillow and stepped inside.

The pillow belonged to Kate. She used to carry it around the house when she was a little girl. I could remember her crying when I tried to take it away from her once. Afterwards, Mom had made me hug her and tell her I was sorry. Even after my apology, she had cried for a very long time.

But she didn't sound anything like the baby that was crying right now.

I didn't want to look at it, so I looked at the pillow instead. The purple teddy bear had been sewn back on recently with black thread. The pillow was dirty and faded. It looked like flesh in the darkness of the room.

The baby kept crying.

I looked around. The place was deserted. Just a chair that leaned to the left because the legs had been cut unevenly, a collection of empty beer bottles, a dresser without drawers, a handmade baby crib.

Ain't no dog, I heard Sonny say.

I leaned my shotgun against the chair.

I forced my eyes to see what was in the crib. My niece. Kate's daughter. She was red, so red I could almost see the heat shimmering off her in waves as she bawled. Her mouth, an open O, sucked in air only so she could scream it back out. Her eyes were squeezed shut. She stank of shit and urine, and I gripped the side of the crib to keep from falling down.

I stayed like this for a long time, and I guess part of me contemplated doing it, and I began to think about things. Things that I hadn't allowed myself to think about in a good while. I thought about Kate and what Pete must subject her to up here. I thought about how I'd like to kill Pete. I thought about doing it now. My hands did not want to burn with that baby's fever. I kept gripping the side of the crib. I kept steadying myself and talking to myself

Once I regained my composure, I picked her up. She burned on my hands just like they knew she would, and she wriggled wildly, kicking me so hard in the stomach that I almost dropped her. Carrying her over to the dresser and peeling off the cloth diaper, I used the clean side to wipe away as much of the mess as I could from her bottom. She screamed at me. I could see her uvula vibrating in the back of her throat.

I picked her up again, squeezing her to me tightly and went outside.

***

Outside, Pete waited, gun in hand.

"Take care of it," he said. He raised the gun so that it was aimed at my head.

"She needs medicine. It's a fever. Some kind of virus."

"I know," Pete said. "It gets worse. Take care of it."

"You can't expect me to—"

"She's going to suffer." Pete was crying now. The gun shook between his fingers

"I can get her help."

"I want that child to die on the mountain. Not in some hospital."

"This what Kate wants?"

"Who's Kate?"

"Your goddamn wife. Is this what she wanted?"

"Sarah said we should get you. I wanted to go away for a few weeks. Leave the sick to tend the sick. Go up in the cove. When we came back it would all be over."

Kate was behind this? And as soon as the question formed, I knew the answer. Yes. She wanted me to come for a reason.

Pete kept the gun aimed at my head. I nodded at him before turning my back and walking over to Kate's horse.

As I walked I tried not to imagine the bullet tearing through my back. I tried to think of Kate. I tried to remember her when she was young, before she changed, before she began disappearing. These thoughts were hard and unsettled me greatly, so I listened to the baby's screams fill the hollow.

I set her on the ground while I untied the horse. She flailed around in the dirt, and I remembered that she was naked. It didn't matter.

After untying the horse, I lifted her into my arms and climbed on. I started back across the trash littered settlement and saw that Pete was still aiming the gun at me. Sonny, meanwhile, had come back outside and was leaned against the doorframe of his house. He was grinning.

I thought somebody might say something else, but nobody did, and even if they had, I wouldn't have heard it over the screaming baby. I left them there, on the mountain and rode all day. When the darkness came, the little girl fell into a feverish sleep and in the silence of the night, I thought about Kate.

◇◇◇◇◇◇◇◇

John Mantooth's short fiction has appeared in *Greatest Uncommon Denominator* (GUD), *Shimmer*, and *Dark Recesses Press*.

Shroud Flash Fiction Contest Winner!

INEXTINGUISHABLE
JESSICA LYNN GARDNER

She could sense this was the right place, the residue of emotion unfolding in layers like the rings of trees. Sparsely clothed saplings and brush had sprouted up through the ghosts of small houses and farms. She walked, trying to cut through the fog of her thoughts. The only thing left of the once-proud churchyard was a crumbling stone staircase far off in the distance. But if she tried, she could see more. The see-through outline of the little cottages, the spire of a church steeple. But there was something that was missing, something else she needed to see. As she approached the ruins, she spotted a small, square house. She entered and slid her fingertips over the rough wooden door.

The sharp points of the splinters in her gnarled fingertips felt so real that she choked back a sob. She stepped through the doorway and into the house, feeling a wash of warmth from the crackling fire in the hearth and the old man squatting before it. He was hard at work, just like he always had been. His busy hands tirelessly worked the stitches through the finely tailored suit material. He squinted at his handiwork and held the fabric closer to the fire.

As the fire leapt toward the flammable cloth she screamed. "Joshua!" He flailed as it consumed him, and the little house was burning to cinders before her.

Tears rolled down as she tried to pull him out, but she couldn't grasp him. She fled out of the open door. When she left her burning home she could still feel the heat; it fed from her and she was a torch of pain.

Three teenagers were outside, but she had never seen anyone dress in such a way. They stared at her, tiny white lights flashing around them. "It's her," she heard one of them say. "The old woman that appears only once a year. Are you getting this, man?"

She dove toward them, enraged at their indecency. They hadn't tried to help him--they let him burn.

They screamed and ran to the far end of grassy plot. She followed, but as she went further out, the shadowy lines began to fade and she was once again amidst the crunching leaves and toppled stones. She approached the teens, but stopped as they stared at a headstone next to two others. She felt the flames engulfing her body douse and with a knowing glance, faded before their eyes, returning to walk the darkness.

With a quivering voice one of the teens read from the weathered stone: "Hannah, wife of Joshua Hanson Died February 9, 1853." Lit with the cold flames of the dead, she relived the death of her husband every year, returning with a soul full of loss and inextinguishable suffering.

∞∞∞∞

A Journalist, Horror/ Fantasy writer, business writer and poet, **Jessica Lynne Gardner** has pursued the art of writing in many forms.

She has published two short stories in Darkened Horizons, an anthology managed by author Jordan Bobe, and another in Word Weaver's Requiem for the Damned horror anthology. "The Second Genesis" appeared in Tome of Distant Realms, a fantasy collection published through Word Weavers. "Seeing Double", will be available October 31st through Twisted Dreams Magazine. Her latest publication,"The Widow's Curse", is included in Sinister Landscapes, a gothic anthology compiled by author of "Bitternest", Alan Draven and forwarded by Andrea Dean Van Scoyoc.

Her work will also appear in two upcoming collaborative projects: The Edward Ballister Project (www.myspace.com/edwardballister) and The Ladies of Horror 2008. She is a member of the International Order of Horror Professionals (IOHP) and Southern Horror Writer's Association (SHWA), and studies at a local college to obtain a degree in literature while writing a fantasy novel and horror stories on the side.

Shroud 4   The Journal of Dark Fiction and Art

WOUNDED WARRIOR
PROJECT

Shroud Publishing and Norman Rubenstein humbly request that you to help wounded service people in their transition back to their lives and families. Whatever your stance on the war in Iraq is, and regardless of your political affiliation, we ask that you take a moment and visit the Wounded Warrior Project Web site to see how you can help those that have made the ultimate sacrifice for our country.

WWW.WOUNDEDWARRIORPROJECT.ORG

Shroud 4   The Journal of Dark Fiction and Art

The Contract

By: William A. Veselik

I met him, for the first time, in a darkened tavern in some city whose name I do not now recall. How long ago it was has also since slipped my memory. It might have been centuries past... or last week. But somehow, neither of those facts matter much to me now.

It was late, near closing time, when I finished my drink and paid my tab. I asked the bartender where the men's room was located and he poked a stubby thumb to my right without looking up from the newspaper he was reading. I wandered to the back of the establishment and followed my nose to the filthy tiled room that masqueraded as a lavatory.

My bladder empty, I made my way back toward the bar, only to have my path blocked by a man's walking stick, ornately carved from some exotic wood. The stick was held by a leather-gloved hand. The hand extended from beneath the sleeve of an expensive silk suit. The man who wore the suit was sitting in a booth, swathed in darkness, and smoking a cigarette. The glow from the cigarette's tip, with each breath of smoke he inhaled, illuminated two eyes that I could have sworn burned like embers themselves.

I've thought many times since about his face, but I have never been able to recall any details. He was handsome, I think, though I could not have guessed his native country or his ethnic origins. His features seemed to ebb and flow with the variation of light and shadow.

His voice was both soothing and unsettling at the same time. There were moments when he spoke in a soft hiss, not unlike a snake, coiled to strike, and the sound made my skin crawl beneath my clothes. Other times, his voice was almost lyrical and pleasing to the ear, the way one imagines an angel might speak, and I craved to hear more. I could detect no accent, not even a distinctive phrase or pronunciation pattern that might have betrayed the place of his upbringing. His vocabulary was refined like that of a man who was well-schooled in literature and the arts, and yet I was sure that he could have bested the world's most bawdy sailor in a cursing match.

I knew he had dined with royalty, caroused with celebrated artists and musicians, and moved in circles of great power and privilege. But I was thoroughly convinced that no debauchery, no crime, no offense against God or humanity was beyond his ability or his experience. He spoke of defiling the innocent, slaying the blameless, and tormenting the righteous. He was boastful of his countless blasphemies, prideful of his innumerable victories, and confident that his evil was both unmatched on the earth and as infinite as the stars.

The very air about him was full of life and I knew he had savored the sweet fruit of human accomplishment for millennia untold. He was no stranger to the theatre auditorium, the concert hall, the museum gallery, or the corridors of academia. It was also apparent to me that he had joyfully wallowed in mankind's filth. He had eagerly embraced every depraved act ever devised by a demented mind. He had applauded each horrid calamity that had befallen humanity. He had spread war, famine, pestilence, and disease as generously as a wealthy man gave alms to the poor. I knew somehow that death was an old friend of his, whose company he preferred and whose work he greatly admired.

But he did not frighten me. I should have been terrified, perhaps, in hindsight.

We talked far into the night, though our entire conversation might easily have spanned mere moments. He told me much. He asked me no questions. He seemed to know more about me than was humanly possible and yet I knew that he, himself, was not human.

He described painful details from my childhood as if he had experienced them himself--an absent father; an alcoholic mother; the terrible isolation of being an only child. He knew the schools of my youth, the names of my few close friends, and every cruel disappointment of my formative years. He seemed almost sympathetic at times, although I detected some discomfort in him. Empathy was a tool of his trade, but it did not come easily. He had to work hard at pretending to care, because it was clear that he simply didn't...or couldn't.

My successful appearance and confident demeanor did not fool him, I think. His eyes pierced façades. His ears discerned the subtle changes in breath and heartbeat whenever temptation caressed the human soul. His cold serpent skin constantly probed the air for warm currents radiated by red-flushed and goose-fleshed human desire. His palate, though jaded by a thousand forbidden flavors, preferred the simple taste of human suffering seasoned with the bitter herb of broken dreams.

He was intimately familiar with the dark foundations of all my deepest fears. He casually verbalized the minutest of anxieties that fueled my greatest worries in life, as though such secretive details were common knowledge among the masses of the world...or at least of the underworld. He spoke of these things as if he understood me on a level that no psychiatrist could have achieved after a lifetime of daily analysis. Yet I could not help but believe he was just warming up to his subject.

"What do you want from me?" I asked him, finally. I was tired of his showmanship and it was obvious to me that he enjoyed the sound of his own voice.

His depthless eyes flashed in anger for a millisecond but he recovered his composure so quickly that I would likely not have noticed his reaction had I looked away for that one instant.

"I fear if I stated that which I seek," he replied, "you might laugh at the very cliché of it."

He blew a cloud of fragrant smoke that wreathed his head like a shadow crown, further obscuring facial features that seemed to swirl and blend with the dark vapors themselves.

I laughed, but the sound seemed hollow and small in his presence.

"Try me," I said, my smile fading.

He crushed out the stub of his cigarette in an ashtray on the table. When I glanced up, another was already lit and hanging from his lip. I'd seen no match flare. He'd made no gesture. The cigarette was just... there.

"Let me just say that I have much to offer you in exchange for...," he paused.

"...for my soul?" I added. He was right. It did sound ridiculous.

"Let us say in exchange for your...loyalty." The corner of his mouth curled in a knowing grin.

"I'm not much of a joiner, you know," I remarked flippantly.

The situation seemed almost ludicrous to me. Here I was sitting in a bar with a man who obviously believed himself to be Satan. He'd have been certifiable in nearly any mental health facility in the country and I was sure that there were white-coated orderlies someplace carrying a straight jacket with my name on it just because I was talking to him.

The only thing that truly made my blood run cold that night was the fact that I believed it, too. I'd seen enough Old Testament movies that I was sure when you were in God's presence you just knew it was God. Burning bushes weren't always necessary. A being with that much power simply could not be denied. Somehow, I figured it must be the same way with Satan. There were no horns, no tail, and no pitchfork, but he didn't need them. He just was.

And, not unlike a corporate executive keen on a friendly take-over, the Devil was ready to negotiate. Half of me was flattered that he considered my soul worth the personal appearance. The other half should have been scared shitless, which I wasn't.

He offered me perpetual health, smirking all the while like a clever snake oil salesman smugly patting his worn leather traveling bag, wherein lay a single crystal vial filled with a shimmering magical elixir.

No doubt the magic potion had been brewed from the bruised leaves of a long-extinct herb by a medieval alchemist who had fallen to dust in his own tomb more than a millennium ago. The elixir was a relic of dark, ancient times. He swore it tasted of damp earth, flesh and sinew, heart's blood. I believed him.

"No disease will ever ravage your body," he promised me. "You will never suffer so much as a sniffle from a mild cold," he added. "You may stroll through the black holes of humanity where pestilence and plague claim their due," he explained, savoring his own vivid description of the horrid places he knew best, "and yet no illness will ever befall you."

He smirked again, the peddler of snake oil making his best pitch to a crowd of one.

But I laughed at his pathetic proposal. I laughed the way a wary man rejects an offer of payment that he knows is barely one tenth of the value of the item he has for sale. No disease would ever harm me, he had said. Not the slightest sniffle. I would live a long and healthy life, unbothered by any of a thousand maladies that might arise to torture and twist the human body.

Then I wondered suddenly, madly and without reason, if Typhoid Mary had ever felt the slightest symptom of the deadly germ she delivered to the world. I doubted it. Would I carry the new plague? Would I be doomed to spread a virulent contagion to my fellow man...perhaps become an outcast shunned in every community on the face of the earth? Or would the virus slay man, woman, child, and beast, leaving me alone to wander aimlessly among the billions of corpses that would litter the landscape.

The catch was there, I was sure of it. And I wasn't going to be caught. I shook my head, but he did not relent.

He guaranteed me fame--as a brilliant actor, a groundbreaking musician, a notable scientist, a great author, the leader of a nation. "It is your choice," he told me. "Children will pledge themselves to follow your example when they grow up," he predicted. "Your name will become a household word, and the people of the world will never forget you as long as there is a world and people in it to remember you," he added.

And he grinned at me a second time. It was the kind of smile that offered no hint of humor. The sight of it caused one's skin to crawl and an unexpected chill to rush up one's spine and prickle the hairs on the back of the neck.

But I spat in his face, though he seemed not to mind the hot spittle striking his cheek. Glistening, it ran slowly down the line of his jaw and hung on his chin for what seemed an eternity. He wore the spittle like a badge of honor. He seemed to relish the feel of it on his skin. I imagined he had been spat on many times before, by men far greater than myself, all of them long dead and gone.

I was insulted that he should think me so vain, but I knew that vanity was one of his favorite sins--one he had exploited with great skill throughout the ages. How many other people had taken his offer, I asked myself. How many actors, musicians, and writers had flown from obscurity to the heights of popularity to die by their own hands—via gun or overdose--or perish in the twisted metal of an automobile on a lonely highway or an airplane in a deserted pasture?

How many scientists had slaved for decades over microscopes and test tubes only to see their discoveries, intended for the betterment of mankind, used for its destruction? Had I forgotten the crimes of Adolf Hitler and his ilk? History was littered with the bodies of self-important fools. I vowed not to be another.

"Pass," I told him, cracking my own humorless grin.

He said he would give me riches enough to glut the Swiss bank accounts of a thousand jaded billionaires. The national budgets of many foreign countries--combined--would tally each year to less than what I received in interest payments on my holdings in any given month. The Internal Revenue Service would be blind to my wealth, he assured me, and no charity organization would ever darken my door.

He dared me to spend all of my cash in a single lifetime and he boldly declared that a pyre made from the money he would give me could not match the heat and flames that the collective nine planes of Hell had to offer. And I was absolutely convinced that he was intimately familiar with the warm climes of those nether regions.

A frown creased my brow for an instant as I considered his offer. That much money could go far in righting the wrongs in my life. I could afford the best homes, the best automobiles, the best clothes, the best food. The burdens of the poor and the destitute of the world could be lightened, thanks to my largesse, and my generous funding of legitimate medical research could no doubt end the suffering of untold millions.

...Or it could make my life far worse. The vast riches he offered might easily become a terrible burden, as I spent every waking hour minding my fortune, counting my pieces of gold, and eyeing the perpetual climb of my stock values. I would never be poor again, I could see, but I might live my life and end my days squirreled away in some counting house.

I could see it in the corner of his crooked grin. He could view the future, surely. He could see how the curse would crush me in its grip. The sun on the grass and the relaxing wisp of a summer breeze on my face would never again command my attention. A soft snowfall at twilight on a still winter's eve would pass unnoticed as I built my empire of wealth. I would give new meaning to the words avarice and greed...and I would die the richest man in the world--never having spent so much as a penny to make myself, or anyone else, happy.

I shook my head slowly. I had little more than the price of a meal to my name. It was enough.

He swore to me that women--any woman I wanted--would be mine, offering themselves to me without reservation, satisfying my most wanton desires and leaving me, willingly, without so much as a single vengeful thought, should I grow tired of them.

Whether I set my sights on a famous actress, a beautiful lingerie model, or simply an attractive young mother at my neighborhood playground, each would welcome my advances without question and never regret her decision. I had but to picture her face in my mind and she would seek me out, wherever I was.

But I casually declined his proposal. I had had my share of women. I had been married once and since widowed. The fairer sex had never beaten a path to my door, but neither had they avoided it entirely. I had never paid for sex, though the thought had crossed my mind on occasion, and the opportunity had sometimes followed soon after.

All the women I wanted.... It was tempting, but what should happen if I found love again. He had not mentioned love. What if no woman could ever love me--only thrash with me in the heated passion of the physical act of love? Perhaps the trap he offered was just that...a life without love. Whether or not I loved any particular woman, she would never return that love. I would always have physical gratification, but never emotional satisfaction. That would be cruel, indeed.

Finally, I realized with a sigh of relief that I had passed each of his tests. I had stared temptation in the eye and had not blinked.

Then he promised me immortality...immortality with health, fame, wealth, and love thrown in for good measure.

And I said yes. God help me, I said yes.

◇◇◇◇◇◇

In **William A. Veselik's** first novel, "Weep Not for the Vampire," Veselik drew from the rural hometown of his youth to craft the tale of a vampire who has come home to lay to rest the old ghosts from his past and to find some method of destroying himself. His second novel, "Corpses So Lively," is the first in a trilogy entitled "My Soul to Take" and was released in October of 2007 by Mundania Press.

OUTSIDE THE LINES
TIM WAGGONER

Cherie was leaning with her elbows on the check-out counter – *Terrorizer* magazine spread open before her, Bad Religion playing on the store's speakers – when the man strolled in. She didn't pay that much attention to him at first. He was a norm, that was obvious from a single glance: late thirties, early forties, red polo shirt, khaki shorts, white socks, running shoes, no tats or piercings. None visible at any rate, and given his age and the way he was dressed, she doubted he had any hidden ones. She figured him for a browser, someone who'd been wandering the mall, saw the store's wares, items made from black leather and gray steel (or plastic made to resemble steel), as he was passing and decided to take a quick walk on the dark side. He'd stroll around the store for a few minutes, maybe give her a smile – if he met her gaze at all – then leave without buying anything. Later, he tell his Stepford Wife and happy clone children all about the freakshow he'd witnessed, can you believe they allow a store like that at the mall?

So Cherie was fully prepared to ignore Mr. Norm and keep on reading her magazine until he left. So when after several minutes he stepped up to the counter and stood there expectantly, she didn't look up right away, figuring he was just checking out the impulse items on display there – kitschy buttons with sayings like EAT DIE AND SHIT, compilation CD's featuring various punk bands, miniature versions of the Dear Dead Dollies . . . But when he didn't leave, she finally registered on her consciousness and she looked up.

"Yes?" She didn't say *May I help you* since she really didn't want to help him. All she wanted was to be left alone until Heather came back from her lunch break and they could resume the conversation they'd been having about Kirk, Cherie's loser-ass boyfriend.

The man smiled as he looked directly at her. He didn't glance down to check out her tits, which either made him a gentleman or gay. Cherie figured gay; it was a safer bet.

"The name of this store . . . Eye-Em. What does stand for?"

There was something odd about his voice, something grating. Cherie wasn't sure what, since he sounded perfectly normal – no surprise – but she couldn't help wincing as he spoke. It was almost as if he were producing some sort of ultrasonic signal that accompanied his words, a signal that she couldn't hear but was nonetheless aware of.

"I'm impressed. Most people who read the sign pronounce it *I'm*, as in *I am*." She thought but didn't say *people your age*. "IM stands for Instant Message. It's a computer term," she added, just in case he really was as clueless as he looked.

His smile didn't waver, not so much as a fraction. In fact, it seemed frozen on his face, as if he were a video image that had been paused. He remained like that for several seconds, and Cherie began to feel uncomfortable. The guy wasn't old enough to be having a stroke or something, was he? But then someone hit "Play" and he started moving again.

"I see. And precisely what message is it that customers are supposed to get – " He glanced down at the plastic name tag pinned to her anarchy T-shirt – "Cherry?"

She narrowed her eyes as she tried to decide whether the man had mispronounced her name on purpose, if maybe he was hitting on her in some weird, clumsy fashion. She pictured his head clamped in a giant vice grip, imagined the handle turning, turning, his eyes bulging out just before his skull popped like a rotten melon. But she quickly thrust the image from her consciousness. She hated it when she imagined sick shit like that. It made her feel all ucky inside.

"It's *Cherie*. And there's no message. It's just a name."

The man looked at her for a moment, head cocked slightly to one side as if he were reappraising her. "So all of this . . ." He gestured to indicate the entire store, the motion of his arm and hand liquid and smooth, like the movement of a well-lubricated machine. "The leather and studs, the icons of death and violence, the atmosphere of irony and mockery . . .

It's all simply, what? Fashion?"

She shrugged. "Yeah, I guess." Realizing how lame that sounded, she went on. "I mean, sure, this is a store and all. But it's not like this is the Gap or anything. This place, the people that buy this kind of stuff, it's all an alternative to the Gaps of the world and the zombies who shop there. It's not plastic, not fake and hypocritical." She wanted to add *like your kind*, but held her studded tongue.

The man had continued smiling the entire time they'd been talking. Now his smiled stretched so wide that the skin at the corners of his mouth tore slightly, and small drops of clear liquid that wasn't blood welled forth. If he felt the injuries, or was aware of them at all, he didn't show it. What did he have, some kind of skin disease? Was he some kind of goddamned leper or something?

"What of the sign on your shirt, that stylized A. Are you a true proponent of anarchy?"

The way this guy talked – the words he chose, the sense of menace beneath them – was at odds with his appearance. And the more she looked at him, the more she thought his skin didn't seem like skin, or at least not *enough* like skin. Its color was too unvaried, and she could see no body hair, no pores. It was as if he were covered in flesh-colored rubber. Mr. Polo. *Condom Man.*

"Well, sure. I guess. I mean, who wouldn't want to live in a world with no rules, a world where you were free to anything you wanted, any time you wanted?"

The man's smile didn't waver as fluid continued to build at the torn corners of his mouth. "You mean a world where anything could happen . . . anything at all?"

Cherie tried not to stare at the growing pearls of serum gathering at the corners of his mouth. "Yeah, why not? It's all about freedom, coloring outside the lines if you want. Hell, coloring off the whole damn page if you feel like it."

A memory of a voice came to her then, mixed with the smells of chalk dust, waxy crayons, and pastels.

Clumsy-fingered little tramp . . . Inside the lines, inside! Or are you too slooooow to know the difference between 'inside' and 'outside'? Would you like me to show you the difference, Cherie? Would you?

Cherie shivered at the memory, and – as if the man were privy to her thoughts – his smile widened a touch more, and rivulets of clear liquid started to run down the sides of his chin. Cherie was beginning to get seriously creeped out now, and when she got scared, she went on the defensive.

"Look, I don't want to be rude –" which was a lie – "but are you going to buy anything or not? If not, I got some stuff I need to take care of in the back." Another lie, but all she wanted was to get out of the man's presence right now, and she'd say or do whatever it took to make that happen.

"Every meaningless day you work here, you're surrounded by the trappings of danger, of life lived on some imaginary edge. But when something truly dangerous happens, you're just as frightened as any norm, aren't you?" Without taking his gaze off her, he reached out and picked up Decomposing Dora, one of the miniature Dear Dead Dollies. "I'll take this."

Cherie just gaped at him for a moment, unable to believe she'd just heard what she'd thought she'd heard. This man, this freakazoid, was lecturing her? She felt like telling him to fuck off, but she figured it would be more trouble than it was worth. It would feel good, damn good, but he'd probably just pitch a bitch to her manager, and while this wasn't the greatest job in the world, it was a hell of a lot better than being a fast-food drone at some greasy burger joint. That was why she took the doll from him and ran its UPC code over the scanner. Not because she was scared of telling him off.

Not!

As Cherie scanned the doll, she imagined wrapping a barbed-wire garrote around Mr. Polo's (*Condom Man's*) neck, twisting the wire, tightening it, the barbs digging into the soft flesh and bringing forth tiny crimson beads of blood.

"Five ninety-five." She glanced at the doll as she reached for a plastic bag with the IM logo on it. The Dear Dead Dollies were a big seller, especially with teen baby-Goth girls. They looked something like the old-fashioned kewpie dolls, cherubic and of indeterminate gender, but instead of a healthy pink their skin was painted gray, green, or white, and they wore tattered, blood-stained clothes. They were four-inches tall, and their features suffered from various malformations – lesions, scars, bloody wounds, stitches, staples – and they all had feral-yellow eyes and tiny pointed teeth. Decomposing Dora had green skin, wiry black hair, and an empty, bloodless socket in place of her left eye. Her black dress was covered with mini-maggots, and ivory bone showed through open wounds on her elbow and knee joints. Cherie thought the doll was cute, in a demented sort of way.

Cherie dropped the doll in a plastic bag and held it out for the man to take. She hadn't seen him reach into his pocket and take out his wallet, but a five dollar bill and some coins now lay on the top of the counter. Without even checking, Cherie somehow knew the coins would add up exactly to ninety-five cents.

The man didn't reach out to take his purchase from Cherie.

"You know, *Cherry*, I'm something of an authority on anarchy. It's my . . . calling, I suppose you could say. You don't *really* understand it, do you? Not *intimately*. Oh, perhaps you did once upon a time, but not anymore. You've forgotten what you learned, and if you're going to work here and wear a shirt like that, it's high time you were reminded, don't you think?" Clear fluid continued trickling down the man's chin, gathering in drops that fell onto his red polo and made dark wet splotches that looked too much like blood.

Cherie didn't like the way he stressed the word *intimately*. There were a lot of norm guys who thought a streak of magenta in the hair, a nose stud, and a black rose tattoo on the upper bicep meant a girl was an easy lay.

She wiggled the plastic bag to draw his attention to it, and in her most formal shop girl manner said, "Your purchase, sir."

Mr. Polo nodded, as if agreeing with a point she hadn't made – or as if he'd come to a decision.

"Tell you what, I've got a few things to do. Would you mind holding on to the doll for me? Thanks." The man started to turn away.

"Wait, we don't do that kind of thing . . ." But it was too late. The man was heading out of the store and back into the mall, moving as swiftly as a speed-walker, and Cherie really didn't feel like chasing after him. She tucked the bag with Decomposing Dora on a shelf under the counter and let out a shaky, relieved sigh, hoping she'd fulfilled her whack-job quota for the day. And hoping that, despite his promise, the man wouldn't come back.

* * *

"It was the weirdest damn thing."

Heather had returned from lunch twelve minutes late, but Cherie was so glad to have her back that she decided not to make an issue of it.

"What was?" Heather was applying a shade of polish to her nails called grave mold. It looked like plain old gray to Cherie.

"That guy . . . the one I just finished telling you about?" Cherie couldn't keep the exasperation she felt out of her voice. Heather could be a bit of a ditz sometimes, but she usually wasn't this spacey.

Heather was a Goth goddess: tall, thin, pale, with bony shoulders and stringy blond hair that always looked stylishly unwashed. She dressed in the requisite black, and favored dark colors for her lips, eyes, and nails. She had no piercings, though. Cherie remembered what Heather had said when she'd asked her about it.

What if I get something pierced and change my mind afterward? It'll be too late then, right? I think I'll just stick with the holes I was born with, thank you very much.

Whatever.

"The guy in the red polo shirt with the weird shit dribbling down his chin, like he had a couple popped blisters or something? Remember?"

Cherie finished her last nail and examined her hands in the store's fluorescent light. "Yeah, he sounds bizarre all right."

From the distracted tone of her voice, Cherie could tell that Heather still wasn't paying any real attention. She sighed and decided to give up on the subject.

"Before I went to lunch, you were telling me the latest about you and Kirk. So . . . what's up?"

It was Cherie's turn to go to lunch, but she wasn't really hungry. Besides, she didn't feel like being alone right now – *especially* out in the mall, where Mr. Polo might still be wandering around.

I've got a few things to do. Would you mind holding on to the doll for me?

She thought of Decomposing Dora waiting under the counter for him and shivered.

"Well, like I was saying, Kirk keeps talking big about putting a band together, but he doesn't play an instrument. Oh, he fucks around on an old guitar he stole from his older brother, but it's not like he can really *play* it." An image flashed through her mind: her grabbing the guitar by the neck, swinging it high, bringing it crashing down on Kirk's head, hearing the hollow ka-thunk of his numb skull caving in. She banished the image and tried to suppress the wave of guilt that followed it. After all, it wasn't as if she'd actually ever *do* anything like that. "I told the doofus that if he was serious about being a musician, he needed to . . ."

Cherie trailed off. Heather had dipped the brush back into the bottle of grave mold nail polish and was now using it to coat her tongue with long, slow, even strokes.

"That shit's not edible. You know that, right?"

Heather stopped and frowned at her. "What are you talking about?" She licked her lips and smeared polish on them.

Cherie felt a twist of nausea in her gut. "You've got to be shitting me."

"You're acting weird. Is your blood sugar too low? You know how you get when you don't eat regular." Heather dipped the brush back into the bottle, raised it up to her face, and began applying polish to her right eyeball. "You should probably take your lunch break." The polish mixed with the fluid in her eye, and a trail of watery grave mold color began running down her face like a sludgy gray tear.

The nausea had given way to a fluttery, panicky feeling in her stomach. "Yeah . . . okay. Sure."

As Cherie walked out from behind the counter, Heather started working on her other eye.

* * *

Cherie headed for the food court. Her entire body was trembling, and she couldn't make herself stop. She was terrified that she might encounter Mr. Polo again – she definitely couldn't handle a return engagement of that whacked-out fuck, not after seeing Heather lose it like that – so she kept her gaze fixed straight ahead, and acted as if she had on a pair of psychic blinders. She reached the food court and grabbed a chair at an empty table. She didn't bother getting anything to eat. She didn't think she'd be able to keep anything down right now.

She tried to tell herself that Heather had just been playing some sort of joke on her, that she hadn't really been using nail polish. It was some kind of new product IM was going to start carrying, something Cherie wasn't familiar with yet. But she knew she was bullshitting herself. She'd seen the grave mold polish before and had recognized the container. What's more, she'd smelled the acrid chemical stink of the nail polish. There was no way Heather could've faked that.

Cherie wondered if Heather had lost it, if maybe she was on drugs or something. And if that had been real nail polish, it could mess up her eyes, couldn't it? She should go back to the store, see if Heather was all right, maybe call an ambulance. Cherie knew that's what she should do, but she couldn't bring herself to get up from her chair, let alone head back to IM. She just couldn't.

She remembered something Mr. Polo had said to her before he left.

You know, Cherry, I'm something of an authority on anarchy. It's my . . . calling, I suppose you could say. You don't really understand it, do you? Not intimately. Oh, perhaps you did once upon a time, but not anymore. You've forgotten what you learned, and if you're going to work here and wear a shirt like that, it's high time you were reminded, don't you think?

It was almost as if he'd been making some kind of promise to her, as if he'd been planning to show her something. To teach her.

So what was she saying? That Mr. Polo had done something to make Heather paint her eyeballs with nail polish? That was crazy!

Almost as crazy as what Heather had actually done.

But Mr. Polo had been wrong. Cherie did understand anarchy, or at least craziness. She'd understood it for a long time.

* * *

Cherie held two crayons – a blue and a red. She was trying to decide which would be the best color for the clown's face. Unable to choose, she decided they'd both look good. She gripped the crayons in her tiny right first, placed the tips onto the paper print-out that Mrs. Galston had given the class, and began coloring in the face of the clown. She had the face halfway finished and was contemplating what colors would look good for the long, skinny, curly balloon the clown was blowing up, when a thick, fleshy hand grabbed her wrist.

Startled, she looked up to see Mrs. Galston glaring down at her. Some of the kids at Kindergarten Town called her Mrs. Gall Stone, and though Cherie understood that was supposed to be a funny name, she wasn't sure why. The woman didn't look much like a stone to her; more like a butter squash that had been left out in the sun too long and was beginning to go soft. Mrs. Galston's face had a yellowish tinge to it, and her puffy flesh sagged, as if she herself was a balloon badly in need of re-inflating. She wore a too-tight, too-old dress covered with a faded sunflower design. Cherie wondered why an art teacher would wear something with such ucky colors.

Cherie had once heard Mrs. Rothchild, her everyday teacher, talking to the librarian about how sick Mrs. Galston had been for the last few months. At the time, Cherie thought it might be something like the flu or strep throat. But Mrs. Rothchild had said the words *brain tumor*, and while Cherie didn't know exactly what that was, she was sure it was something really bad.

"What do you think you're doing, young lady?" Mrs. Galston's voice was high-pitched, with an accompanying rattle that made it sound as if she had plastic buttons caught in her throat.

Cherie tried to answer Mrs. Galston, knew she would only get in more trouble by not saying anything, but she couldn't make herself talk. Mrs. Galston terrified her, and she wished art period was over and she was back in Ms. Rothchild's class. Mrs. Rothchild was nice, and she never yelled or grabbed, not ever.

Mrs. Galston tightened her grip on Cherie's wrist until it began to hurt. But even though there was a whimper of pain somewhere inside Cherie, it refused to come out. The art teacher's doughy-slack features wrinkled into a scowl, and she leaned down closer to Cherie's face, as if she thought the girl might be deaf.

"Look at what you've done."

The teacher's breath smelled like rotten eggs and cough syrup, and Cherie thought she might gag. At first she didn't know what Mrs. Galston was talking about, but then she saw that the woman's gaze was fixed on the picture Cherie had been coloring. Cherie examined the picture to see what was wrong with it. It wasn't finished, of course – she'd only just started when Mrs. Galston had come over – but otherwise she couldn't see anything wrong with it.

She turned back to Mrs. Galston, and though she still couldn't bring herself to speak, her confusion must've shown on her face, for the teacher said, "The colors are all wrong. A clown's face should not be *both* red and blue . . . and what's worse, you've gone *outside the lines*." Mrs. Galston said this last part as if she were naming one of the worst crimes imaginable, like stealing cookies or fibbing to your mother.

Cherie turned her attention back to her picture. She had gone outside the clown's face, but only a little. She couldn't see what the big deal was. Besides, she kind of liked the way the red and blue squiggly lines didn't quite stay inside the clown's face. It was like he was growing red-and-blue whiskers.

Cherie was trying to work up the courage to ask Mrs. Galston to please let go of her wrist, 'cause it was really, really, *really* hurting now. She imagined the art teacher releasing her, then saw herself taking the two crayons she'd been using – the red and the blue – and shoving them up Mrs. *Gall Stone's* nose . . . shoving them so far up that the tips poked into her brain and burst through the tumor that was growing inside her.

But despite her fear and anger, Cherie wasn't able to get her words out. It didn't matter, though, for Mrs. Galston finally released her grip without Cherie having to say a word.

"Clumsy-fingered little tramp . . . Inside the lines, inside! Or are you too slooooow to know the difference between 'inside' and 'outside'? Would you like me to show you the difference, Cherie? Would you?"

Cherie didn't dare look away from Mrs. Galston, but she sensed the other children in the class watching her. She could feel their fear as well as their cruel joy at watching someone other than themselves get in trouble.

Cherie finally managed to croak out a single word. "Please . . ."

"So you *do* want me to show you? All right." Mrs. Galston stood, walked briskly over to her desk, and snatched up a pair of scissors. Not safety scissors, but grown-up scissors – black metal handles and long sharp silver blades. The teacher hurried back over to the table where Cherie was sitting. Tears were starting to run down Cherie's face, but Mrs. Galston gave no sign that she noticed. When she spoke next, she sounded calm and reasonable, as if she were teaching a lesson.

"Right now, Cherie, my blood is on the inside of my body." Mrs. Galston opened the scissors, placed one blade against her left wrist, and drew it across her skin with a single, swift stroke. Blood sprayed from the newly opened wound, splattering onto Cherie and stippling her partially finished clown picture.

Mrs. Galston smiled serenely at Cherie. "And now it's on the outside."

As blood continued to spurt like a fountain from Mrs. Galston's wrist, Cherie found her voice at last and screamed.

* * *

"Hey. Heather said I'd find you here."

Cherie's head jerked up with a start. Kirk stood there smiling, a slightly bemused expression on his face. He pulled a chair away from an empty table, put it down opposite Cherie, and sat. Normally, that was the soft of casual, offhand rudeness that irritated her about Kirk. He didn't ask if it was okay if he joined her, didn't ask if she felt like company. He just sat the hell down. But right now she'd never been so glad to see anyone in her life – until he spoke, that is.

"So, what's the problem? Heather said you were acting really weird."

Kirk was shorter than Cherie, and a little on the beefy side. He used to shave his head, but now his scalp was covered with fine brown stubble. He claimed he was re-growing his hair so that he could go for the 80's "big-hair rocker" look. Cherie didn't know if he was kidding or not, but she sure as hell hoped so. He wore black pants, boots, and an old Ramones T-shirt. Like his guitar, he'd stolen the shirt from his older brother. Cherie didn't know if Kirk had ever actually listened to the Ramones, but she doubted it. He sported a scraggly goatee that refused to fill in, large metal "studs" in both ears (he refused to call them earrings), and thick, black jagged line tattoos that encircled both wrists. Seeing them made Cherie think of Mrs. Galston slicing open her wrist with the scissors blade, and she felt hot bile splash against the back of her throat. She swallowed and then, fairly confident she wasn't going to barf, started talking in a rush.

"*She* said I was acting weird? You should've seen what she was doing when I left! Wait a minute, if you talked to her, then you know. You saw her, right?"

Before Kirk could answer, an Asian woman approached their table. She was in her early thirties, Cherie guessed, and wore the uniform of a "Wok This Way" employee. She carried a brown plastic tray on which sat a small Chinese take-out container.

"Excuse me, but would either of you like a free sample?" the woman asked, a hint of an accent in her voice.

Cherie wanted to tell her to fuck off, but Kirk had never met a food that he didn't like – especially when it was free. He stood up and peered into the open container.

"What do you got?"

"Today's special is pierce my nipple with a toothpick," the woman said with a cheery smile.

Cherie couldn't believe she'd heard right, but Kirk reacted as if the woman hadn't said anything out of the ordinary. "Sounds good!" He reached into the take-out container and removed a wooden toothpick. The woman put the tray down on the table in front of Cherie, and Cherie could see that the container held nothing but toothpicks. Dozens of them. With deft, sure motions, the woman unbuttoned her uniform blouse to reveal small breasts with erect brown nipples.

"Would you like right or left, sir?" the woman asked, still smiling.

Kirk thought about it a moment. "I don't know. Which would you suggest?"

"Left," the woman said. "The nipple's a bit bigger there. You'll have a larger target."

"All right."

Cherie watched in numb fascination as Kirk pinched the woman's left aureole and with a single swift motion, as if he were baiting a hook or threading a needle, jammed the sharp toothpick through the nipple. Blood spurted, and the woman took in a hissing breath that was a sound half of pleasure and half of pain.

Kirk stared at the blood dribbling from the wound he'd just created. "That was fun." He turned to Cherie. "You want to do the other one?"

Just like all those years ago with Mrs. Galston, Cherie couldn't make her voice work. She stood and backed away from the table, shaking her head.

Kirk shrugged. "Your loss." He reached for another toothpick, and as Cherie turned to run, she heard the woman draw in another ecstatic hiss of air.

* * *

Fuck. This. Shit.

Cherie didn't know if the world was going crazy or she was, and she really didn't care. All she wanted was to get the hell out of the mall as fast as possible. Once outside, she'd run and keep running until either her legs gave out or her heart burst. Right now either would be fine with her, just so long as she was away from here.

As she ran through the mall corridors, she tried to keep her psychic blinders up, but she couldn't shut out the images she saw. A fat woman holding a toddler with his face buried in her stomach flab, arms and legs flailing as he smothered. A group of people standing outside a sporting goods store, inserting fish hooks into the naked flesh of an old man who kept shouting, "Deeper, dammit, deeper!" Another group of people inside a pet store, skinning animals with their bare hands, eating the meat and wearing the bloody pelts like hats. And there was more, so much more, but it all merged into a twisting, swirling kaleidoscope of blood and madness. But just when Cherie thought she never would reach the exit, that maybe there *wasn't* an exit any longer, she rounded a corner and saw the central fountain – water spraying into the air to splash back down into the marble basin filled with water, at the tiled bottom a scattering of coins tossed in by people who didn't really believe in wishes but couldn't help themselves. The mall's main entrance lay just on other side of the fountain. She'd made it! She'd –

Cherie stopped running. Standing in front of the fountain, between her and the exit, was a clown. Red shirt, rainbow pants held up by orange suspenders, overlarge brown shoes, white pouch slung over one shoulder. His shirt wasn't just red, she saw, but a red *polo*, and his face – a face she'd seen in IM only a short while ago – was now covered by a mass of red-and-blue squiggles, as if he'd been tattooed in crayon.

The man, the clown, the whatever-he-was saw her, grinned, and waved.

"Hi, Cherry! Told you I had some things to do!"

He reached into his pouch and pulled out a slender purple balloon. He stretched it a couple times, put it to his mouth and began filling it with air. The balloon expanded, lengthened, and the tip split into three separate tendrils. Mr. Polo continued blowing, and the tendrils kept growing, writhing away from him as they became increasingly longer, as if possessing life of their own. Then the tendrils reared up as if they were serpents and lunged toward a trio of nearby shoppers: an elderly man on a motorized scooter, a pre-teen girl wearing a Johnny Depp T-shirt, and a pot-bellied guy dressed in a light-blue work shirt and tie. The balloon tentacles wrapped around each of the trio's waists and hoisted them into the air. The scooter fell out from under the old man as the balloons, with a strength and force they couldn't possibly possess, lifted the three over the fountain and slammed their bodies together over and over again until the were reduced to limp meat bags filled with shattered bones. The balloon-tentacles then released the bodies and they dropped into the fountain. Water splashed, and Mr. Polo – balloon now out of his mouth, end pinched tight so no air would escape – looked at Cherie and grinned.

"Make a wish," he said.

Cherie ran like hell toward the entrance, hoping that if she moved fast enough, she could bypass Mr. Polo and make it past the fountain – without looking at the bloody, broken ruins that had only a few moments ago been three human beings. She didn't know if she'd be any safer outside than inside – what if the whole fucking world had gone nuts? – but it didn't matter. She couldn't take any more of this
insanity.

"Not so fast, Cherry!" Mr. Polo put the end of the balloon back in his mouth and started to blow once more. The three blood-smeared tentacles shot straight toward Cherie like rubbery missiles. With the speed of striking snakes, they encircled her waist once, twice, three times, and, though filled with nothing more substantial than air, held her in a grip like iron. She could no longer run, couldn't move, could barely even breathe . . .

Slowly, the balloon tentacles began to pull her back toward Mr. Polo, and though she tried to resist, they drew her inexorably on until she was standing right next to the psychotic fuck. Though her arms were pinned to her sides, she imagined they were free and pictured herself reaching into his pouch, pulling out a handful of limp, empty balloons, and jamming them into his mouth, shoving in one handful after another, until the crazy sonofabitch choked to death.

"That's right, that's the stuff . . ." Mr. Polo's eyes gleamed with a wild light, and he practically purred his words. "You create such lovely mental images, Cherry. When I first sensed them, I knew you were just like me: a hungry-hungry worm gnawing his way through the sweet, fat apple of creation. When you were in kindergarten, Mrs. Gall Stone taught you the most important lesson you ever learned: that anything can happen at any time, and it all means dick. You were gifted with a great insight into the true nature of existence, Cherry, but you turned your back on it. You denied the truth and became like them . . ." He gestured at the crowd of people that thronged the mall. No longer were they lunatics that attacking or mutilating whatever moved. They had returned to their normal banal selves. Near-mindless creatures whose only purpose in life was to spend money, eat fast food, hold empty conversations on cell phones, and send meaningless e-mails with smiley-face icons after every other word.

"Worse than them, really, for you acted as if you were above them, as if you and your pathetic little tribe of Halloween-costumed playmates were the only ones who knew what true darkness was. You did know once, Cherry, when you were baptized by the blood of an insane kindergarten art teacher dying from an inoperable brain tumor. And when I wandered into your store and saw the delicious dark images in your mind . . ." He trailed off and smiled. "I thought I'd do you a favor and remind you of what you'd forgotten, sister. So, what's it going to be? Are you going to force yourself to forget your lesson again this time, make it go away and be never-was? Or are you going to finally embrace the truth and become what you were always truly meant to be?"

Cherie stared into Mr. Polo's gleaming eyes for several moments. She thought of Mrs. Galston, of the clown picture with the red-and-blue squiggles on its face, of Heather, and Kirk, and her dull-as-fuck job at IM. Then she smiled and raised a hand that had been empty a moment ago, but which now held a pair of black-handled scissors.

"What do you think?"

* * *

Heather was just about finished applying a second coat of grave mold nail polish to her fingers when Cherie came back from lunch.

"Did Kirk find you?" Heather didn't look up as Cherie approached the counter. "I told him you'd probably be at the food court."

When Cherie didn't answer, Heather scowled. "What's wrong? Need a refresher course in manners?"

Shroud 4   The Journal of Dark Fiction and Art

"I've already had my refresher course for the day, thanks."

There was something odd about Cherie's voice. It sounded normal enough, but it grated on Heather's ears, made her wince as if she were hearing fingernails being dragged across a chalkboard.

"Would you like to hear what I learned?"

Heather finally looked up, blinking painfully as she tried to get her sore eyes to focus. She wondered what was wrong with her vision. Was she was starting to get sick or something? Maybe. That would account for the awful taste in her mouth, too. She decided she would stop off at urgent care after work.

"What are you . . ." Heather trailed off when she saw the lopsided smile on Cherie's face and, though she wasn't sure, it looked like Cherie's eye-blinks were no longer in sync. There was some kind of oozy red glop on her T-shirt, too, crimson smeared across the A for anarchy.

And she was holding a pair of scissors.

"Today I learned about the difference between inside and outside. Let me give you a demonstration." Cherie raised the scissors and stepped around behind the counter.

* * *

Cherie gazed down at her handiwork which lay on the floor, surrounded by a widening pool of blood, a pool that was definitely outside. She was satisfied; it looked just like she'd pictured it.

She dropped the scissors onto the body, then reached beneath the counter and took hold of the plastic bag that she'd placed there earlier. She didn't want to leave Decomposing Dora behind. After all, her new friend had paid for her.

"The three of us are going to have a lot of fun, aren't we, Dora?"

Cherie . . . no, *Cherry* walked out from behind the counter and headed into the mall, thinking of all the wondrously dark pictures she and her friend were going to bring to vivid, blood-soaked life.

◇◇◇◇◇◇

Tim Waggoner wrote his first story at the age of five, when he created a comic book version of King Kong vs. Godzilla on a stenographer's pad. It took him a few more years until he began selling professionally, though.

Overall, he's published over 70 stories of fantasy and horror (some of which are newly available at Fictionwise) as well as hundreds of nonfiction articles.

In addition to writing fiction, Tim has worked as an editor and a newspaper reporter. He currently teaches creative writing at Sinclair Community College in Dayton, Ohio, and in the MA in Writing Popular Fiction program at Seton Hill University. He has two bright and beautiful daughters.

Tim hopes to continue writing and teaching until he keels over dead, after which he wants to be stuffed and mounted, and then placed in front of his computer terminal.

Malcolm McClinton

Flash Fiction Contest Honorable Mention

THREE GRAVES
BLU GILLIAND

There they were.

They'd been on the move again, but he'd found them. He always did.

"Right this way," he called over his shoulder. Crashing through the underbrush behind him was the family he'd met at the campground. "Sorry it was such a hike, but like I told you, they move around."

The three – a man, his wife, and their son – emerged from the thicket and stood beside him.

"That's them?" the man asked.

"Yep."

Sunshine fell across the three tombstones, illuminating thousands of tiny cracks wrought by a century of nature and neglect. The boy went straight for them, running his hands over them, sending small chunks of granite tumbling to the ground.

"Edgar!" his mother cried.

"He's fine," the guide said. "These stones have survived a hundred years of wind, rain and animal piss. He ain't gonna hurt 'em."

She frowned, but said nothing else.

"So what's the story with these?" the man asked. "Maybe it's 'cause we're out here in broad daylight, but I gotta be honest – this place don't feel haunted to me."

"Place isn't haunted," the guide said. "The graves are.

"See, back in 1902, the bones beneath these stones were a family much like yours. The Hansons. Had a little cabin in the woods. Lived a quiet life, raisin' a boy just like Edgar here.

"One night a man came knockin' on their door. Problem was, he did his knockin' with an ax. The family escaped into the woods. Hid out for two weeks with that fella on their tail the whole time, snortin' like a wild boar and choppin' down trees. He caught 'em when they went back to their cabin for food. They thought they'd lost him, but he was as good a hunter as he was crazy. Slaughtered 'em on the spot."

"Why'd he go after them?" the man asked.

"No reason."

"And these graves..."

"Originally stood behind the cabin. But not long after they were laid to rest, they disappeared. Been spotted all over these woods in the years since. People say the family's still tryin' to hide from their killer."

"I think we'd better be getting back," the mother said.

"One more thing," the guide said. He reached under his flannel jacket and pulled the hatchet out from where he'd tucked it in the back of his waistband. He stepped over to the man, who was examining Hannah Hanson's tombstone, and buried the hatchet between his shoulder blades.

"NO!" the woman screamed. Edgar fled into the woods.

The guide pulled the hatchet from the man and wiped the blade clean. The woman never tried to run. She just went on screaming until the first blow landed.

"Did you listen to the story?" he screamed into the woods. "I'm a good hunter!"

He turned back to the three graves, all of them now decorated with dark splashes of blood.

"Don't go anywhere," he said. "You know I'll find you. I always do."

⋄⋄⋄⋄⋄

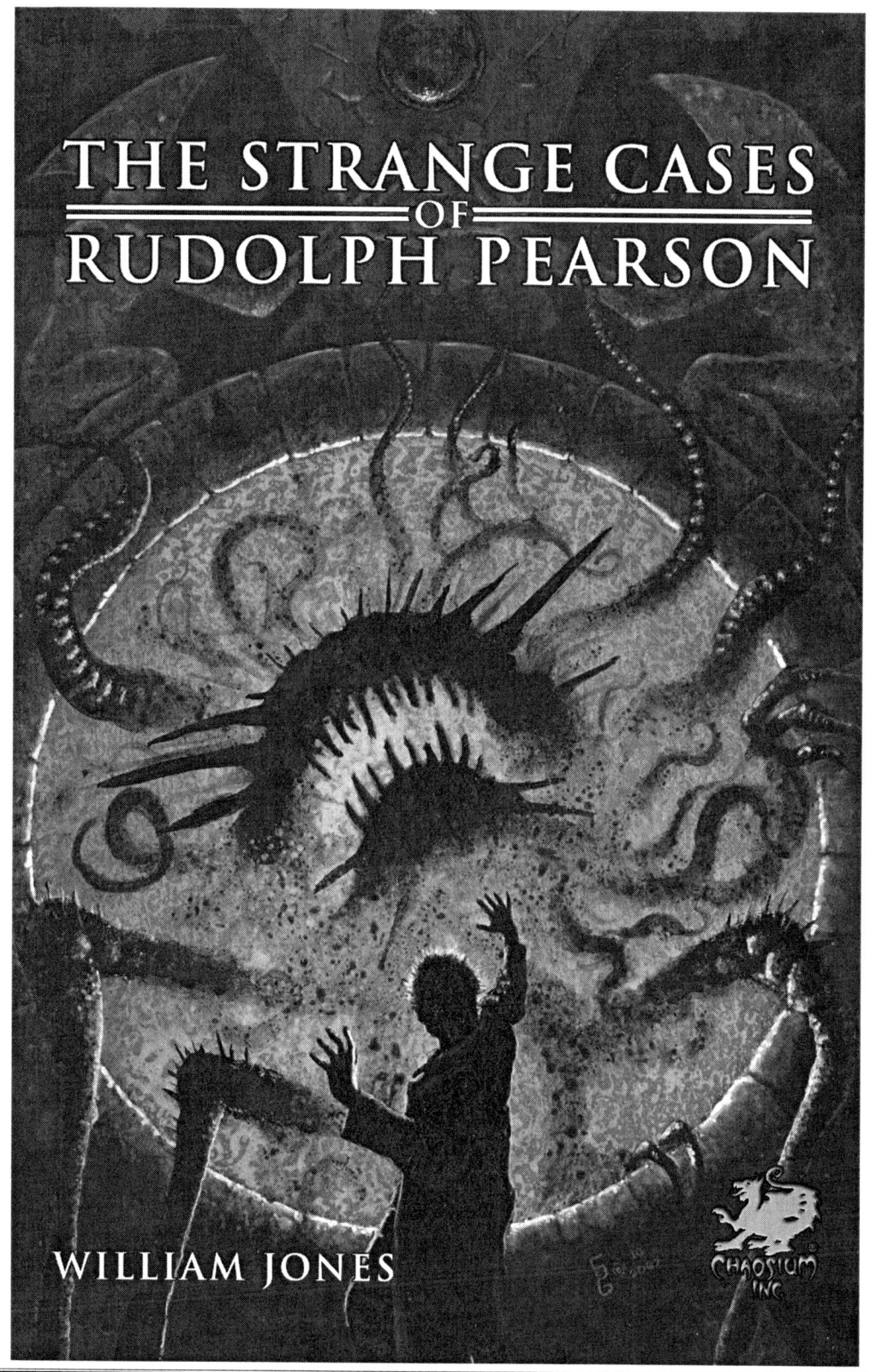

Your Horror Collection Would be in Ruins without Shroud.

Visit Us Today

www.shroudmagazine.com

Books, Magazines, More

Sketch of a Ruin

Michael J. Deluca

"No one can deny his personal merits as a traveler, his enthusiasm, boldness, acuteness, courage in danger, and perseverance under difficulty. ... Of Central America and her antiquities Mr. Stephens may know, and no doubt does know, as much as the most learned antiquarian. Here all is darkness."
-- Edgar Allen Poe, Review of John Lloyd Stephens' *Incidents of Travel in Central America, etc., Graham's Magazine*, August 1841

September 1840. Jungle near Valladolíd, Yucatán, México.

The roar of the approaching conflagration was like a multitude of screams. The wall of fire reached forty feet into the air, and the rich green of the Yucatán jungle turned ashen in its light. The foliage, starved for moisture as the dry season neared its end, writhed in hot wind and ignited before the flames had even touched it. Low clouds blanketed the night sky, passing swiftly west. Their undersides glowed red.

I had chosen a seat against the frescoed wall of the overgrown temple such that I could watch death coming, watch the hellish glow that fell between the crooked columns and across the limestone floor. My fingers, wishing for a sketch pad, finding none, occupied themselves probing the crevices in the crumbling stucco, furthering the decay of the lost civilization that Stephens and I had traveled fifteen hundred miles to document. I couldn't stop myself.

A decayed, man-shaped altar reclined beside me at the center of the chamber. *Chacmool*, the natives called such figures: a deity of rain. Its face, beatific, seemed prepared for death, as though I'd taken refuge from the flames atop a dead god's long-awaited pyre. Chiapa Chi stood hunched over the stony figure with a brush, scouring centuries of sediment and mold from its folded hands, its lap, its upraised knees. The black hair knotted atop her head, the concentration fixed on her blunt features--they were the same she wore every morning, fixing her masters their juevos and juice. But the flowers on her dress were torn and stained, and a dozen opulent necklaces swayed over her lumpy bosom: the flicker of gold, the glint of tanzanite and jade—intricate carvings echoing the patterns in the walls, faces within faces, each iteration more grotesque than the last.

A rasping, labored breath, as though the stone god had woken, and John Lloyd Stephens stumbled into the temple, stooping low to fit beneath a lintel made for men of lesser stature. His body radiated the berserker-strength with which he had so often attacked our labours of discovery; even Chiapa Chi left off scrubbing to gaze on him. Black ash streaked Stephens' trouser-legs and boots. His shirt hung open to his heaving chest; his skin glistened, covered in a labyrinth of bloody scratches, like the scrawling of ignorant men aping the writings of the wise. Stephens flung down a machete crusted with the gore of jungle vegetation. He fell into a fit of coughing.

I tried to think how long he had been gone. What had happened in that time? Where had my own mind been? From beyond those mad, skewed columns, the vision and the voice of hell intruded on my thoughts. I remembered waking from siesta to Chiapa Chi's insistent shaking. Smoke stinging my eyes. A flight through the jungle. Behind us, machetes swing against the sunset, torches, angry shouts in the staccato native tongue. Our own workmen had betrayed us, set fire to the jungle. Why?

A heavy rucksack slid from Stephens' shoulder; he rummaged inside, spilling its contents: a crushed sombrero, a pistol, a meerschaum pipe, two bedrolls, a sheaf of maps and sketches whose casing he tore in his haste. He drew out a water-gourd, wrenched away the cork and drank.

"I've cut a firebreak," he managed, stifling his cough. "We won't burn to death... perhaps cook instead... though chances are the smoke will suffocate us first." He cracked a smile I refused to accept. Even the monumental endurance and daring of John Lloyd Stephens had to have a limit. Yet his false optimism spurred me to guilt. My fingernails were cracked and bleeding, caked with earth. Had I simply been cowering here, while Stephens fought to save us?

I lurched to my feet and reached out to him, seeking... what? To absorb some part of his incredible vitality and thus overcome my own fear? "John. Why didn't you rouse me?" I stammered.

"Be still, Frederick." Stephens set aside a sack of cornmeal. "You're weak from the fever. Sit down."

Bare weeks before, I had hovered on the brink of death, mad with fever wrought by the vapors of the tombs. On death's brink--but never closer than this. I could see death over Stephens' shoulder, stalking us. The wall of the inferno couldn't have been fifty yards away. "I can widen the firebreak," I blurted. "I can save us." And I lunged across the scattered gear for the machete.

Stephens interposed his body between me and the door. "You'll only kill yourself the quicker." The determination in his eyes made me shiver. "Besides—I need you here."

His work clearing the ruins had all but ceased while I lay sick. He told me he couldn't continue without me: my skills as a draughtsman, my pragmatist's eye. Delirious, I believed him. It was this, as much as Chiapa Chi's infusions that gave me strength to recover.

Since then, I had regained my sense of what was real.

I lowered the machete, let it drop. I couldn't best him, even in his exhausted state. When he saw I didn't mean to try, he returned to the pack without a word.

The torn sheaf of sketches rolled towards me, stopped against my foot. "Our work," I said. "Your book. My sketches. The things we've seen—now the world will never hear of them."

"All our successes, our ambitions," said Stephens, "will seem but self-aggrandizement, compared to what we are about to achieve. Though," he added, "only we will ever know of it."

With a cry, he produced from the pack a fist-sized bundle of cloth. He explored its contents as a man would test a limb for broken bones, and a clear, screw-topped specimen jar slipped into his palm. The sight of it, here, shook me more than I can say. In the glow from the entryway, its amber contents appeared to clutch at the glass, at the flesh of his hand pressed against it. The effect was that of a living thing, held in suspension for centuries, arisen, ravenous.

I drew in a steadying breath. The notion was insane—a remnant of the fever, a product of the inexorable heat. Stephens, it seemed, had begun to take leave of his senses. The smoke and exertion had been too much; he lacked the experience of fever, fighting off delusion. I must remain objective, for his sake as well as mine.

Honey. That eerily translucent, golden substance was nothing but the nectar of some unknown flower, collected and converted to sugar by the servants of an insect queen, then harvested by human hands and sequestered away for an eternity in the kingdom of the dead. Our Indian workmen had discovered it that afternoon, in a clay jar that cracked when they broke too clumsily through the ceiling of a tomb. They had recoiled from that spreading stain, fled into daylight like lizards disturbed from their lair. Only Chiapa Chi had held her ground. Indeed, she recognized the honey before either of us: she knew it by the scent.

"The honey," I muttered. "Is this why they turned on us? But why? The Indians--they only come here for the work, for the means to feed their families. Why would they seek to murder us, their patrons?"

Stephens' eyes flicked towards Chiapa Chi.

The revelation struck me like a blast of heat. *It was Chiapa Chi who led us to this temple. We would never have found it on our own.* And Stephens--Stephens had followed her.

The muted features of the stone idol, the *chacmool*, were aloof, serene. Thanks to Chiapa Chi's meticulous attentions, the rain god's rigid figure glowed a burnished white--save for the place in its lap, below its folded hands, where the black stain of sacrifice would not be removed.

Chiapa Chi wouldn't look at me. I caught her by the wrist. The skin at the heel of her hand was calloused from months spent rolling tortillas to feed hungry and exhausted men. Her forearms were thicker than my own. The myriad faces in the jade stones strung across her bosom shone with vile anticipation. I reached for them, meaning to rip them from her throat. "If you wanted the honey so badly, why didn't you steal it like everything else?"

Stephens' hand closed on my shoulder. "Frederick, don't you see she's put herself in danger for our sake?"

Outside, the flames were closing, eating up the ground. Smoke seeped in below the lintel, filling the room with gray haze. My eyes watered. "We're going to die. You act as if a drop of honey is worth that!"

Chiapa Chi wrenched from my grasp. She spat into the rain god's lap, scoured the wad of moisture into the stone. "*No estoy ladrón. Son ustedes.* You are the thieves."

Stephens' brows gathered above his aquiline nose; his ash-smudged mustache curled. He looked...as he had always looked. Noble. Self-sacrificing. Heroic. "You don't understand what this is, Frederick." He held the jar of honey like a talisman, his knuckles white against the gold. "You're right: it won't bring us fame or fortune. It may not protect our bodies from the flames. But that isn't why we came here. You know how much I sacrificed to finance this expedition. I've staked my life, my reputation. Bartering with rebel factions, bribing church officials--I've lost count how many thousands of acres of trackless jungle I've bought and paid for at twenty times their worth. I consider it money well spent. Don't you? Your illness, Frederick--hasn't what you've learned been worth that? Chiapa Chi placed herself in the firestorm's path, not because she hoped to throw her life away, but because of what she hoped to gain."

He fell into another fit of coughing, his passions having outgrown the capacity of his flesh.

Chiapa Chi shouldered past me. She stooped over the scattered contents of Stephen's pack. The pistol caught my eye, silvered barrel winking in the firelight. If she had brought us here to die for her gods.... I grabbed it out of her reach.

She tucked the sack of cornmeal into the crook of her arm, and then pressed the water-gourd to Stephens' chest.

He took a long draught, groaning with relief. Then he gave her the gourd and the honey jar. "Tell him," he said, gasping. "*Cuentale de la miel.*"

Chiapa Chi pursed her wrinkled lips, and then spoke reluctantly. Her accent was not Spanish, though her words often wandered into that tongue. "*Las Quichés, se llaman ayahuasca. 'Soul's rope', we say. It is a tainted honey, made from nectar of a sacred flower, extinct in Yucatán por sietecientos años.*" She retreated to the altar.

Stephens pawed for the pistol, closing his hands around my own in such intimate fashion that I had to release it. His voice rasped in my ear. "You understand? Soul's rope: an umbilical cord, connecting man to the gods. Left behind in a tomb. That honey was these people's gate to heaven."

I remembered fevered dreams: the sun-scarred features of the work crews turned monstrous, ringed about in the blinding noon with strange mosaics; crescent-eyed demons pawing at the canvas of my tent; birds with leering monkey faces swooping to make off with drafting tools I later found among my bedding.

I looked over the vastness of the Yucatán obscured by fire, trying to reassure myself with my senses. Trying not to think what kind of heaven might have awaited the architects of the civilization on whose ruins we stood. Fearing I already knew. The inferno would reach us in minutes. I imagined quetzal birds and jaguars burning, their spiritual might unable to persist, faced with such incontrovertible proof of the primacy of the physical plane.

Stephens thrust out his jaw. "Consider the Spaniards--<u>they</u> came to Yucatán seeking riches and renown. And they found it. When the conquering force made land, the natives threw away gold in the streets and fled with chocolate instead. The natives didn't care for wealth. Certainly, they valued gold less than life. The Spaniards laughed at their simplicity and exploited it. As a result, the name of Cortés is known throughout the world, while these people have been utterly forgotten."

The foliage at the edge of the firebreak wavered, distorted by heat. The air was acrid, the breeze searing. Tears streamed down my face.

"Wealth and fame," said Stephens, gasping, "are not the ultimate commodities. Life has greater value than gold. But life too is ephemeral. Experience is what makes life worthwhile. Enlightenment, Frederick. Enlightenment is beyond price." Stephens flung the pistol through the doorway. Spinning end over end, it arced down into the flames.

I choked upon a cry of loss. The gun had offered the shadow of control. With it, I could have cut short his illusions, put an end to this madness before it became...whatever it was about to become.

I took the sheaf of sketches to the corner by the lamp, sat on the grimed, cool floor, and unrolled them across my knees. Here were represented more than eighteen months of work, documenting the ruins of a lost civilization unknown to the world. My life's greatest achievement, soon to be ashes. My last chance at detachment.

Native workers clearing the steps of a temple at Tuluum. Stephens smoking a pipe in the courtyard of the Caracol at Chichen Itza. The House of the Magician at Uxmal: a hulking temple like a hunched man crowned in stone. Stephens again among the ruin of Izamal, hunting panther under the vacant gaze of a megalithic god.

The last sheet was blank. I found a charcoal pencil in the pocket of my shirt.

The shapes came instinctively, circumventing thought. My breathing slowed, as did the thudding of my pulse. I sketched the architecture first, the low doorway, its columns and primitive lintel, the altar's placid posture. Then I turned to the frescoes: feather-crowned, jaguar-faced warriors parading rank-on-rank around the walls, fading in and out of existence as they marched across centuries of decay. Only when these were complete did I bother to outline the living figures, capturing posture, a hint of body language, nothing more: Chiapa Chi's squat intensity, mixing her porridge of water, ground maize and apocryphal honey; Stephens' towering, almost satirical straightness, staring out at the flames. Myself, as always, I left out of the scene.

It was too late to alter Chiapa Chi's posture on the page when she straightened regally, whispering in her native tongue, produced a paring knife from her bosom, pulled back the ruin of her dress and slashed open the inside of her thigh. Fat raindrops of red marred the surface of the *chacmool's* fresh-cleaned lap. More spilled into the porridge. Her face did not register pain; if anything, it became still more beatific.

"*¡Ven acá!*" she said. "You both must sacrifice."

"You're going to die, Frederick," said Stephens. "We all are. She's only offering a chance to save your soul." Stephens pushed up his sleeve. His jaw clenched as Chiapa Chi bled him.

"Go to hell," I said.

He winced, buttoning his shirt cuff tight over the wound. "I need you with me, Frederick. I need your objectivity. You are my foil. You keep me honest."

He loomed over me. I raised the sketches like a shield; he was too quick. His bloody hands closed around my collar. The pencil slipped from my fingers. I made a fist and swung at Stephens' jaw.

An otherworldly screech. A fiery shape hurtled in through the doorway, an incarnation of the vengeful anger of the flames, the dead god whose tombs we had defiled. Stephens flung himself out of the burning thing's path. I fell atop the sketches. It crashed into the wall above my head and spun away, fluttering and screaming. I glimpsed broad wings trailing fire, a wild eye rich with color, blind with agony.

Stephens lunged up like a cat. His arm swung through the smoke. There was a ringing, metallic thump. The bird struck the wall a second time, and then dropped to the floor. The flames that had robed it in the semblance of power died away, leaving it withered, featherless—no demon, no phoenix, but a parrot, lost in the inferno.

"Enough," said Stephens through clenched teeth, pressing his wounded wrist to his side. "Frederick, do as you're told."

I rolled the sketches tight. Asked myself what was a little more pain. Considered which part of my body to offer in defeat.

"No time," said Chiapa Chi, suddenly between us. The conflagration's roar intensified. A wave of heat brought us to our knees. Beyond the mad, skewed columns, there was nothing but red.

The tip of her knife shot out, so quickly I had no chance to react. A bead of blood rolled down my knuckle and fell into the porridge.

Chiapa Chi flung up an arm to shield her eyes and darted through the doorway. She set the gourd of honey porridge on the temple stoop, bare yards from a cliff-face of flame. She stumbled back cradling a seared and bubbling hand, half her face scorched red.

Stephens tried to help her. She pushed him away, binding the burned hand in a length of cloth ripped from her dress.

I crawled after them into the meager shelter of the altar, hugging the sketches close. We knelt around the bird's carcass, heads low to the ground, watching through slotted, stinging eyes as the fire snapped at the temple walls and the skin of the gourd peeled and charred.

Every breath I took seared my

lungs. My tongue was swollen, sandpapery and raw. Stephens began to cough. "How long must we wait?"

"Not long," said Chiapa Chi, and advanced a second time into the inferno. The glare obscured her from our vision.

When she returned, she had transformed into a demon, like the bird. The black smell of seared hair and burned flesh assaulted us. Half the hair was gone from her scalp. Her blistered cheek and brow were like a lizard's yellow scales. The cloth fell from her burned arm in cinders, exposing a blackened claw. With her remaining hand, she cradled the gourd in the tatters of her dress.

How could she keep her feet? Even if she'd deluded herself to believe what she'd told Stephens--to believe it fiercely enough to turn his mind--how could mere belief drive such determination?

Chiapa Chi dropped the gourd into the altar's lap and split it apart with a blow from the machete. Inside was a near-perfect little honey cake, golden brown and steaming, barely charred. With incredible care and precision, she split the cake into three equal slices, using the back of her destroyed fist to steady the machete's blade. Then she scraped together the leftover crumbs and the last of the honey and spread a little on each one.

"Pues, don Stephens, don Catherwood, por favor, a cenar."

She smiled weakly. We were all about to burn, and here she wanted us to dine on ashes.

As Chiapa Chi chose a slice and devoured it, and Stephens struggled to overcome a new fit of coughing long enough to do the same, I shrank to the floor before the altar, overtaken by delirious, hiccupping laughter. She truly did believe it: that a cake made from honey seven centuries old could be a passage to the spirit realm, to the wisdom of her ancestors, whose golden visages dangled at her breast and surrounded us upon the walls. She had given her life for this chance. And, beyond reason, she had offered the same chance to us.

"Why?" I asked her, gasping. I reached up, caught her unburned hand, the calluses, the heat radiating from the skin. "Why would you share such sacred wisdom, not with your own people, but two arrogant white men?"

Chiapa Chi swallowed. "My people rob their own ancestors' graves at the bidding of white men. For centuries, the Spanish rob them. Now Americans rob them. My people don't know what they have lost. El caballero–don Stephens–*por lo menos el quiere comprender.* Without him, the honey would never be found."

I lay back, closed my eyes. My head was strangely clear. Illusions of clarity—I had known such moments during fever. They had always come before the worst.

Then, at the nape of my neck, unmistakable, I felt it: a breath of cold air, damp, as from the crypt. The altar's base--there was a gap, a crack between the human figure and the floor!

Stephens held the poison cake in his fingers, halfway to his lips. I struck it from his hands; it flew into the flames. He reached after it feebly.

"A crypt!" I shouted, clutching him. "God damn you, John--a crypt! A passageway, beneath the altar. Help me. We can live!"

His eyes were bloodshot, his breathing indistinguishable from the roar of flame.

The hair on the backs of my arms had been singed away. In moments, this temple would become an oven. The last of the air would be gone before that.

Alone, I dropped to one knee before the altar. I thrust my shoulder against the stone—I, Frederick Catherwood the invalid, a weak and sickly man, undertaking to rip from its foundations a monument that might have stood here for millennia. I forced my body taut. I strained with muscles, tendons, sinew, pushing against that man of stone as though seeking petrification. The jagged contours of the chacmool's limestone crown dug deep into my palms. I imagined myself wrestling with the god.

The altar gave. It tipped at the base and for an instant teetered, threatening to fall back upon me and crush out my life. Then it pitched back and struck the floor with a shudder.

I don't know how I achieved it. All I knew was that the yawning, creeping black that opened at the altar's base meant life.

The last slice of honey cake, the one Chiapa Chi had meant for me, spilled from the chacmool's lap. Drawn by the promise of the grave's unsullied air, a gout of fire burst through the temple door.

With a cry, Stephens lunged into the face of the oncoming flame, pawed for the cake and stuffed it whole into his mouth.

I caught him by the belt and hauled him back. Fire had caught in his clothes; I beat it out with my hands. There was too much smoke to speak; I don't know what I could have said. I didn't know if the poison cake would kill him or transform him into some ravening ghoul. But he was my friend, and I owed him my life.

I heaved him towards the toppled altar. He stumbled backward over it, slammed his skull against the limestone, and slid, limp and boneless, down into the darkness.

I scooped up the roll of sketches from the floor, smothered the smoldering edges against my chest. A stride away across the fire-filled temple, Chiapa Chi was a squat, blurred figure clothed in a mantle of umber and crimson, her expression as calm as that of the broken altar. It brought to mind an image from the sheaf of singed papers I held in my hand: the stele of the sorcerer-monarch at Copan.

I dove into the crypt.

In the space between life and afterlife, I had the time to blink, to observe the red rectangle of light receding above me. Then the lumpy softness of Stephens slammed into my chest, knocking the wind from my lungs. Blissful coolness enveloped me, save for the pain where my burned skin touched Stephens' body.

I pushed myself tottering upright, on ground that rolled and rattled beneath me. No doubt I was standing on skulls, on precious artifacts and nests of scorpions. I flung out my arms, but found nothing. I fell.

A croak from above, inhuman, emotionless, dragged my gaze upward.

Chiapa Chi stood there, framed by the hole where the altar had been. My eyes may have deceived me, incapable of compensating for such absolute contrasts. Certainly I was closer to madness than any fever could have brought me. But I swear I saw her skin char, her flesh shrivel away, her pendants and necklaces melt, liquid gold dripping like honey over deep green jade. And whether the last gasp of destroying air that escaped from Chiapa Chi's lungs was meant as a reproach for stealing Stephens from her, or a cry of despair at having her illusions torn away, I could not guess. The voice was that of death.

Poisonous monsters laired in these catacombs, even if demons did not. I could hear them, skittering, slithering to bask in the heat that seeped through the walls. We might yet die here; we were trespassers, living men hiding in the kingdom of the dead.

I couldn't bring myself to care.

* * *

Stephens stirred before I did. He groaned and sat up, his shape barely visible in the flames' reflected light. I wondered if he might mistake this place for heaven.

His hands moved around him, exploring. His fingers brushed my ankle. I recoiled, dragged myself away. I might have crawled like that forever—there no walls to stop me--save that something hard and chitinous moved beneath my touch. I clutched my hands to my chest, felt my wrists for the poison wound that would kill me.

Stephens crawled to my side. I felt his breath, smelled a sweetness. A taint.

"Keep away from me," I said.

The sound he made, I think, was laughter, hoarse, filling the black space that surrounded us. "You weren't always a coward, Catherwood. What put this fear in you--the fever? Why couldn't you be satisfied to crawl into this grave and hide from enlightenment—why did you have to drag me with you?" Rough hands closed upon my throat. "You've no idea what you have robbed me of... what you could have had yourself."

"Chiapa Chi is dead," I croaked. "She didn't ascend. I saw her body wither. You call that enlightenment?"

His grasp tightened. Scarlet stars burst across my vision, utterly unlike those of flame. "You didn't see what happened to her soul."

My sketches. I had dropped them. I didn't fear death at his hands. What I feared was oblivion. I felt for them frantically, finding only limestone, earth, and bone. I clutched at his arms. "What did I steal from you?" I asked. "I saw you eat my share of cake. All I did was save your life."

He dragged me backwards into the light. The burning temple's glow revealed a face like some sacrificial mask, discoloured with burns, stained by blood, darkened with rage. And yet it was no demon, no resurrected god. It was Stephens.

The pressure on my windpipe slackened. He withdrew into shadow.

I found the sketches at the very limit of my reach. I hugged them to me. "You meant to trick me into ritual suicide. When I refused, you tried to compel me. And when I saved you from your self-sacrificial design, you would have murdered me outright."

"It's true." His voice was hollow. "I... I called you a coward. But I couldn't face death without you. To meet heaven alone would have meant nothing. How could I know what I had become, unless I saw it through your eyes?"

The red rectangle of the shaft overhead burned into my corneas, leaving behind a stain in green. "You helped me through my fever--I thought I owed you my life. But you never meant to let me keep it."

"Forgive me, Frederick." He kicked something. It rattled, clicking as it rolled end over end. "But I wish you'd let me die."

"And you talked of enlightenment," I said.

"You don't understand." His face

was close again; I smelled the honey's sweetness on his breath. "The gift of honey, the soul's rope—it was only meant for those already dying, to guide them past the brink. To living flesh, it is a poison. I feel it working. Changing me. I can't withstand it."

He began to pace, muttering, cursing, himself or me I couldn't tell, three strides away, then three strides back, halting every time at the edge of the shaft's red glow. What delusions did the tainted honey show him in that dark? Over the crunch of bones beneath his feet, the skittering of vermin could be heard: the worker bees of the underworld, carrying the ash of souls like pollen on their shoulders, away into storage among endless terra-cotta jars, there to age a thousand years awaiting the death of an unborn queen, or king—or hero.

If he wanted death, all he had to do was walk. Lose himself in the unknown.

But John Lloyd Stephens was no hero. He'd found the limit of his ambition, the point at which high-minded dreams must yield before mortality. A limit I'd found weeks ago.

"Did you ever wonder," Stephens asked, "what would happen to us when the book was complete? I mean after the fame, the praise, the museum exhibits, the lecture tours. Once it faded, what else could we do? Lost civilizations, from now on, will be discovered only by men like Poe, in lies."

I went after him, pulled him away from the dark. I made him sit beneath the shaft. I wrapped my arms around his shivering flesh.

I had saved his life already. It was too late to take that back.

* * *

That night, I witnessed John Lloyd Stephens laid low. I listened to him screeching, groveling in abjection before absent idols, pleading with nothing, hurling accusations at gods who had revealed themselves only to him. He confessed to all the lies he'd told himself, the oaths he'd broken. I knelt beside him, in a quicksand made of bone dust, piss and vomit, fighting to keep him from drowning in guilt. Twice he begged me for his pipe, three times for water. I had nothing to give him.

Stephens sought the ultimate commodity: enlightenment. He gave all he had to achieve it.

Finally the red rectangle faded to blackness. Stephens, shivering, covered in sweat, having expelled everything that was in him, lay his stained cheek on the fouled floor and slept.

I could not.

* * *

After how many hours, the rectangle began to glow again: faint blue, then gray, then rose. I shook Stephens awake. My face, after a sleepless night spent in the grave, must have looked as horrible as his. His pupils had narrowed to pinpricks; the surplus of iris granted his gaze a reptilian cast—but the tips of his moustache curled in relief.

After a time, he got to his feet. I laced my hands, and Stephens stepped into them. I hoisted him up, my arms trembling. His weight lifted away.

I waited, wondering what he saw and how the soul's rope might distort it. The corpse of Chiapa Chi. The blackened remnants of the jungle. A sky bleak with smoke. The underworld we had defiled exacting its revenge by creeping out upon the living.

"Help me up!" I shouted. He didn't answer.

What might have been wind roared through the shaft; I mistook it for the rush of blood through my heart. The sketches were impossibly heavy. Circulation in my limbs had slowed from sitting still so long; it felt as though my legs had been replaced with swarms of bees. I was afraid.

Then Stephens' hand thrust through the hole. I shoved the sketches in my shirt and jumped to catch his grip: firm, though clammy and still shaking.

The *chacmool* lay where it had toppled. Stephens' pack and our possessions were smudges on the floor. No sign remained of Chiapa Chi—not even jewels. We stooped to pass beneath the blackened lintel.

A moist wind, laden with the scent of charcoal, pressed our clothes against burned skin. The stones were slick. Scattered columns of rain angled through a broken sky.

"Do you see it?" Stephens asked. "I see a ruined city, risen up out of the earth. Is it real?"

The jungle landscape was transformed. The earthen mound on which our temple stood, its dense coat of fern and thorn consumed away by fire, had become a stark pyramid of limestone. Across a waste of black mud punctured by the bones of trees, dozens of such structures surrounded us--lesser pyramids, combed temples, carved monuments, colonnaded courts.

There are limits to the reach of reason, as well as to the ambitions of heroes.

I withdrew the sheaf of sketches from my shirt. I felt my pockets for a pencil--then remembered it had burned.

Sound traveled strangely over

that altered landscape. Distant voices, hushed with awe, reached us as though whispered in our ears. A score of Indians slogged single file across the mire, covered to the waist in ash, craning their necks to take in the vision of that resurgent acropolis.

It was our workcrew. No one else had cause to venture so deep into the jungle; anyone coming from Valladolíd in response to the fire could not yet have arrived. These were the arsonists--the men who had betrayed us.

Catching sight of us, they erupted into argument. The leader pulled off his sombrero, mopped his brow. *"Chiapa Chi,"* he shouted. *"¿Que pasó? ¿Como la chingada sobrevivieron? ¡No lo creo!"*

The wind gusted. A tendril of the breaking storm battered my singed and brittle clothes with rain. There was a choking gasp from Stephens, and then he was wrenching me around to face the temple door.

There, framed by the columns, naked but for necklaces, stood Chiapa Chi. Her body was whole and unburned, painted the colors of sky, mud and limestone. Her arms were folded. Her expression—I could never read that sun-scarred, foreign face--but I thought she was laughing at our surprise. She spoke, but her words were obscured by a rumble of thunder. Without sign or warning, she disappeared.

The Indians debated, gesturing at us, at the sky, at the massive feathered serpent stela that had appeared out of the jungle's ashes at the pyramid's foot. Then they ran.

The thought flickered across my mind, like lightning, that, death being inevitable, transcendence just might be preferable to notoriety among thoughtless men.

When the sheet of rain and our betrayers had fled, Stephens came awake, as from a trance. He asked me if I'd seen what he had seen—Chiapa Chi, arisen from the dead.

I lied, to spare him. And myself. Still, he insisted we venture back into the temple, lift the chacmool from where it had fallen and set it aright.

> "I see a ruined city, risen up out of the earth. Is it real?"

"As we passed along the edge of the milpa, half hidden among the cornstalks was the stately figure of Chiapa Chi. She seemed to be regarding us with a mournful gaze. Alas! Poor Chiapa Chi, the white man's friend! Never again will she make tortillas for the Ingleses in Uxmal! ... The sun and rain are beating upon her grave. Her bones will soon bleach on the rude charnel pile, and her skull may perhaps one day, by hands of some unscrupulous traveler, be conveyed to Doctor S.G. Morton of Philadelphia."

--John Lloyd Stephens, *Incidents of Travel in Central America, Chiapas, and Yucatán*, 1841

◇◇◇◇◇◇

Michael J. Deluca describes himself as a writer, reader, dreamer, designer, photographer, philosopher. Would-be ecoterrorist. False prophet. Liberal.

Flash Fiction Contest Honorable Mention

OFFERINGS
DESMOND WARZEL

When she'd come to him and told him, smiling her devilish smile, that she wanted to try doing it in a graveyard, he'd had immediate misgivings, fueled by long-dormant memories of campfire tales that had recounted, in earnest and vivid detail, the gory consequences of this particular trespass. Even so, he never seriously considered turning her down for two reasons: first, she had always been a real sport about accommodating--with genuine enthusiasm--his every tentative suggestion in the bedroom; and second, he knew just the graveyard for it.

The place was untouched and practically untouchable; there were no headstones less than a century old, and the overgrown road leading there had been practically impassible for his jeep. It would have stranded a lesser vehicle upon its jutting rocks and upthrust roots.

Their lovemaking was awkward at first; the ground was uneven, the vegetation masked numerous rocks, and the thorny foliage scratched at any carelessly flung extremity. Still, the forbidden pleasure of their act quickly eclipsed their minor physical discomfort, and good sex was made great.

He awoke alone the next morning. Her clothes were still scattered about, but she had gone; most likely into the surrounding trees to relieve herself in private.

When she hadn't returned in half an hour, he dressed and searched the woods in ever-expanding circles, but found no trace of her or her passing.

Once back in town, he made inquiries--gentle, subtle--but none of her friends or relatives had seen her that day.

In his apartment he paced, sometimes stopping to stare at the discarded clothes he'd laid out on the sofa, as if he could somehow will her into them.

After dark, he drove back out to the graveyard, for there was no getting around it. She couldn't have run off naked, and an intruder's vehicle would have awakened them. He saw only one explanation.

Their desecration of the graveyard had attracted the angry attention of its residents. They had come in the night and taken her back with them as an offering, compensation for their disrupted slumber.

For the second time he pulled the jeep into the clearing. He picked up the sledgehammer from where it rested on the passenger seat. His mind burned with a dozen fevered images of the unknowable place they had taken her; he pictured dark places, and places all too well-lit.

Teeth clenched, he smashed the headstones, one at a time. With aching muscles and patience born of inevitability, he gathered the slabs together. A hundred graves desecrated; a hundred lives erased.

In the center of the graveyard a truncated staircase went no place, the long-abandoned start of an unbuilt crypt. He piled the broken stones neatly around it.

He had their attention now. They would take him to where they had taken her. He would rescue her, or he would spend eternity there beside her.

He climbed onto his makeshift altar and lay down, watching the stars overhead and waiting for the dead to come.

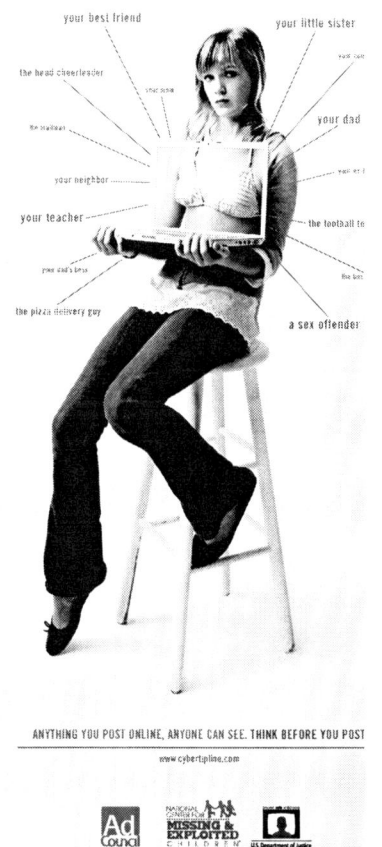

LAURA

BY J.F. GONZALEZ

Naomi stepped outside to get the morning newspaper when the man jumped out from behind the porch retaining wall and grabbed her arm.

"Don't scream," he said in a hissed whisper. He gripped her arm tightly. "I'm not going to hurt you if you don't scream."

She held back a scream. His grip on her arm tightened, and she caught a glimpse of a handgun. "Okay, we're going to walk to the front door of your house. You aren't going to do anything funny. We're going inside. Okay?"

She nodded and felt the tears come. The hot summer sun beat down on her face and she had to struggle to keep from crying. A thousand thoughts ran through her, but the most important one was keeping him away from Laura, her daughter.

"Let's move," he said.

Nudging her firmly, he escorted Naomi back up the driveway to the front door of her house. He kept the gun on her, shielding it from possible sight from neighbors with the cover of his body.

Naomi's key ring was still in her hand, and she automatically inserted the house key in the lock and turned it. The door opened, and he ushered her inside and closed the door behind them.

The sound of the lock engaging felt like the lid of a coffin slamming shut over her.

The curtains were drawn over all the windows, shrouding the house in darkness. As if he knew the layout, the man ushered her through the foyer into the family room. He pushed her towards the worn sofa and pointed the gun at her. "When's your husband get home?"

She got her first real good look at him, and despite the fact everything was happening so fast, she was able to see that he was a big man and had a look of desperation. "I... I don't... please, don't hurt me..."

"*When* does your husband get home?" His tone was more demanding, more desperate.

"I... I don't have a husband," Naomi said, the words slicing through her as they came out. Even now, after two years, it still hurt to talk about Larry and what happened to him. "It's just me."

"Don't lie to me!"

"I swear, it's just me!" She fought to keep the panic out of her voice. "Please, don't hurt me, I swear I won't tell anybody, I won't tell – "

He pointed the gun at her. "Get up!"

"What?"

"I *said*, get *up*!"

She got up.

"Come." He motioned for her to follow him. Naomi followed him, her nerves too shattered to do anything else now.

Once in the kitchen he started opening drawers. "You have duct tape?"

"Y.. yes," she said. "First drawer on your left."

He found the drawer and opened it. He pulled a roll of duct tape out and regarded her for a moment. "Turn around and get on your knees with your hands behind your back."

Trembling and crying, she did as she was told. She slowly lowered herself to her knees, ashamed at herself for crying but not able to stop it. She hoped that whatever happened, it happened fast and Laura wouldn't get home until it was all over and the man was gone.

Please God, get this over with, please just let him tie me up and ransack the place, let him take whatever he wants to feed whatever addiction he has, he can rape me if he wants to but please don't let him still be here when Laura gets home.

She felt rough hands grab her wrists and begin binding them with the duct tape. She doubted he was in possession of the handgun still – she wouldn't think he'd be able to bind her like this while armed – but she imagined he'd set it down close by. No way in hell was she going to try making an escape in this position. He had the upper hand.

When he was finished binding her hands behind her back, he stood up. "Okay, on your feet. Come on."

He guided her back to the living room toward the couch. "Sit down."

She sat down on the sofa. He was

looking around the room, as if casing the place. He was a good-looking guy, perhaps in his mid-thirties, with black hair and tanned skin. He appeared to be in good physical shape. He was dressed in black jeans and a black t-shirt and white tennis shoes. Aside from the handgun he was brandishing, there was nothing about him that stood out.

Keeping the gun trained on her, he backed up toward the French doors that opened onto the backyard patio. He peered through the blinds. "Where's the bedrooms?"

"Down the hall," she said. Her stomach was doing slow flops in her belly.

"You have a shower I can use?"

"Yes."

"Where were you going?"

She decided to be honest and tell the truth. "I was going to the store for some groceries."

"You have a job?"

"Yes." A lie, but what he didn't know wouldn't hurt him.

"What do you do?"

"I'm a child psychologist." It was the first thing she could think of, especially when it came to dealing with Laura.

This seemed to affect him. He fidgeted with the gun, his left hand rubbing his face. "A child psychologist, huh? Just what I need. Jesus."

Naomi didn't know what to say. Everything had happened so fast. Had she said the wrong thing?

He picked up the roll of duct tape he'd left on the kitchen counter and placed the handgun down. He pulled out a strip of duct tape. "What about kids?"

"No kids," she said quickly, hoping the lie wouldn't backfire. *Do whatever you came here to do and then get out, just leave!*

He knelt down in front of her and began binding her legs together at the ankles. "I'm not going to hurt you," he said. He tore off the long strip of duct tape that now bound her legs together and pulled a smaller strip off. "I need to use your shower and clean myself up a little. Then I need to rest. Okay?"

She nodded. She wondered if he was running from something, or if he'd committed some kind of violent crime. "I'm gonna tape your mouth shut so you can't scream, and then I'm gonna use your shower. I'll leave the TV on, okay?"

She nodded again, feeling a tear slide down her cheek.

He picked up the remote control and turned on the TV. There was a commercial for some fast-food restaurant on, and he turned back to her. "Okay?"

She nodded again and he taped her mouth closed and left her there, bound and trussed up, and went down the hall to the bathroom.

A moment later, she heard the shower start up.

The commercial ended and the news came on.

Her captor's face loomed large on the screen. In the background, a popular, local newscaster reported what was being considered a major story. "...shot and killed a hospital security guard, identified as forty-eight year old Herb Eckman, as well as twenty-nine year old Carol Whitman, who was identified as a Hospital Administrator, when a nurse tending to his four-year old son, Henry Oliver, found the suspect in his room attempting to remove the breathing tube – "

Her eyes grew wide as the story rolled on. She could only sit up in rapt attention, the suddenness of the story overwhelming her.

"...Greg Oliver had fled when officers arrived at the home he shared with his wife and young son. His wife had called 911 saying Greg tried to drown their son Henry in the bathtub. Despite attempts to fight him off and save Henry, the boy was unconscious when Mr. Oliver fled the scene. The child was rushed to UC Irvine Medical Center where he was listed in grave condition. A bulletin was put out for Greg Oliver's arrest, and he remained undetected until this morning when he showed up at the hospital and managed to sneak past security. When Emily Bacon, a Critical Care Nurse who works in the Pediatric Unit, walked into the ICU, she saw Greg attempting to remove his son's breathing tube. When Mr. Oliver attempted to flee, Mr. Eckman tried to stop him. That's when Greg Oliver opened fire with what appeared to be a nine millimeter handgun."

Naomi watched the news coverage in stunned silence as Greg Oliver showered down the hall.

She learned the rest of it quickly. Greg had fled in a white Camaro with the police in close pursuit. Greg had abandoned the car five miles away, in the development she lived in, and there was no trace of him. He was also the father of a two-year old son, Bobby, now deceased. His wife had been arrested but was never charged with his death, which had been labeled an accident.

The sound of a helicopter flying over eclipsed all thought and broke her attention from the newscast. The police were here, at her subdivision, conducting a search.

Down the hall, the shower stopped.

She felt tense as the news droned on in the background. There was no doubt that if the police showed up while Greg Oliver was in the house, he would kill her. But if it took another few hours for the search team to reach this end of the subdivision and Laura –

Laura! What would happen with Laura? Would her elementary school let the kids out of school knowing what was going on?

She worried about this while the news coverage continued, and before she knew it Greg Oliver was standing in the living room dressed in a pair of Larry's old jeans and nothing else, towel-drying his hair as he watched the TV.

After watching the coverage on himself for a few minutes he muttered, "Goddamn. They didn't waste time putting this on TV, did they?"

She didn't say anything; her heart beat heavily in her ribcage. She felt sweaty, hyped up with adrenaline.

Greg turned to her. "They're searching the development?"

Trembling, she nodded.

The shower seemed to have reinvigorated him. When he'd first taken Naomi hostage he'd been primed up, on the edge, a man driven to desperation. She'd seen the tiredness in his eyes. Now the shower seemed to have driven away whatever fatigue he'd had; he looked more dangerous now than ever.

They watched silently as the news anchor brought the viewing audience up to speed, repeating the story she'd seen earlier.

Naomi stayed silent, watching him.

Finally, he turned off the TV with the remote. "Okay, this changes everything. Damn!"

Her thoughts were running a mile a minute. She shook her head, hoping she'd see the look of desperation on her face. He looked at her for a minute, and then reached over and ripped the duct tape off her mouth. Naomi winced at the pain, debating on what to tell him. "It's only ten-thirty," she said. "It's not going to take all day to canvass the area. They'll probably finish by two and reopen the development. When they do that, you can go. I'll even drive you out myself." *Then you can go and be out of my life, she thought. Before Laura gets home.*

He was shaking his head. "They're not going to reopen it so soon," he said. "They'll keep it closed off. They'll escort people into the development as they come home from their jobs. They're not going to write me off as being gone so quickly. They know I'm nearby somewhere."

"Well, they can't just <u>force</u> their way into every house in the neighborhood," she said.

"I dumped my vehicle only four blocks from here," he said. He regarded her calmly with those dark eyes, that strangely passionate and dangerous face. She noticed for the first time that he was lean, his stomach flat and hairless. "They're going to concentrate their attention four blocks in either direction. That means they're going to mostly be smack dab in the middle of this development."

"If they do, we just won't answer the door," Naomi said. "We'll just –"

Greg tore off another strip of duct tape from the roll. "I'm taping your mouth shut again so you don't scream when that happens." He leaned forward, ready to tape her mouth shut again when she shook her head.

He paused, irritated. "What?"

"Why…" Naomi began. *Go ahead, ask him!* she thought. With that little bit of internal courage, she finished her thought process. "Why did you try to kill your son?"

He looked at her for a moment, his dark eyes deep and penetrating. "So you want to know why a man would go out of his way to kill his own child?"

She nodded. She had to gain his trust, and the only way she could do that was to keep him talking, learn what made him tick, empathize with him. In that position, he might let down his guard enough to allow her to --

"You want to know what you're up against, huh?"

She nodded again.

"Bet you see a lot of cases of kids with behavioral problems, don't you? Kids who are out of control; not in the normal sense, but more than you'd expect."

"I suppose I do," she said, playing along with him.

"Bet these kids' parents don't know what to do with them, do they? They come to you because they think you have some insight into their child's behavior. They think because of all your big degrees and your years of practice that you have some insight into what makes a child's mind work. And you know what?"

"What?"

"For the most part, they're right." He leaned forward and placed a rough, callused hand over her mouth. His voice was a whispered hiss, his face inches from hers. "Here's where your colleagues have got it wrong, though. *My* son's a little monster. Everybody always says that children are special, children are our future, they're innocent, but it's all bullshit! There are birth defects and there are mental abnormalities. We see them every day and we live with them. Sometimes we can treat them. But out of all those physical and mental abnormalities there's an even smaller percent, maybe less than one percent of all those kids born with certain deficiencies, that have something <u>else</u>, something that makes them <u>different</u>. I don't know what it is, and

I haven't been able to find anybody that can help me, not any scientist, or doctor, or psychologist. Nobody! All I know is what I've seen, what I've experienced, what I've seen happen around me and my son. He's a monster, and he'll grow up to be a bigger monster if I don't do anything about it! He'll–"

"What has he done?" She didn't realize she was going to ask this question until it was out of her mouth. She shuddered, hoping she'd said the right thing.

Her question startled him. Greg looked at her, his eyes wide. His breathing seemed to stop. He still had his hand over her mouth but it loosened somewhat, which was how she'd been able to ask him her question. Now the hand relaxed slightly. He was looking at her with a false sense of hope. "What are you saying?" he asked. "How do you know?"

She felt elated, and sagged with relief at the sound of his last question. She had the necessary background to deal with this, and it was more than enough to deal with him!

"If this is some bullshit," Greg continued, his hand still over her mouth, "I'm not buying it. I know what I've seen and –"

"I know what I've seen too," she said, the words coming out in a rush. "I see it all the time in my practice and believe me, what you're saying is something I've been turning over in my mind now for the last few years. I know society puts children on a pedestal, that children have become poster things for politicians and clergymen, that so many of our laws and the way society is structured is to protect children. You want to know something? It's all designed and manipulated by these ... these things that aren't children. They're the ones manipulating parents into becoming shrill overbearing advocates for child protection at every level of society. And they do this because it drops our guard against the real threat – the creatures who are masquerading as children!"

"I don't know if I should believe you," he continued. "You probably think I'm psycho or something, saying shit like this about kids. You're a psychologist, you're probably just stringing me along and — "

She shook her head. "No, I know what you're talking about. Believe me, I've seen it enough in my practice that—"

His eyes narrowed. "There's pictures of a little girl all over this house. Who's that?"

"My sister's daughter," Naomi lied. She could tell he believed her, and she continued. "I don't have kids and I'm not married. My husband, he wanted children, but I didn't. I … didn't have time … I wanted to concentrate on my career. That's why we broke up." Another lie, but what he didn't know wouldn't hurt. "My sister has a daughter and I guess she's a good kid. She sends pictures every few months. I have pictures of other people in the house, too. Didn't you notice them?"

He nodded now, the suspicious expression slowly giving way. "You asked me something a minute ago," he said. "You asked me what my kid did, as if you knew he's done something … that he's not like other kids. How did … why'd you ask that?"

Naomi's answer came quickly. "Because I know children are born with no conscious, no sense of morals, of right and wrong. Most parents do a good job of raising them and instilling some sense of values in them, but a lot of them don't even bother. It becomes easy for such children to become emotionless vacuums. I've read stories about pre-schoolers who snap suddenly and lash out violently at playmates, of elementary school kids shooting each other at school and not even feeling sorry for what they've done. It's something I've taken interest in, something I've read up on since I was in my early twenties when my parents, my whole family actually, started asking me those pesky questions about when I'm going to reproduce. They wouldn't accept my reasons for wanting to be childless. They felt there was something wrong with me for not wanting to be a mother, especially since I work with kids. Personally, I don't see anything wrong with self-preservation, for not wanting to reproduce. A child in the womb is a parasite, a leech draining a woman's natural resources. When it's born it physically depends on the mother for nourishment. Likewise for the father if he decides to stick around. The father becomes a host mostly on the financial end, but also the psychological. His life suffers to a degree. Most people can handle that and even like it. I knew early on that wasn't for me. I didn't want that kind of drain on me, so I opted to not have kids." She paused for a moment, watching his reaction. "Society doesn't encourage this, though. The way everything is so... so..."

"Child friendly?" He asked. He removed his hand from her mouth.

"Yeah." She nodded.

"That's part of what they do," he said. Naomi could tell she was getting to him now, that she was getting him to let down his guard and trust her. "It's their trick. They've been fostering this notion that breeding is good, that the more kids people have, the more emotionally fulfilled you'll become. They do this because they want more of themselves. They're rare, you know. Only a fraction of all births in the world. That's tiny, a drop of water in a vast ocean. There were more of them up until the last fifty years or so. Now people wait until their thirties and later to have kids. And the things don't *like* it. That's why we're seeing such an increase in the way they're manipulating those in power to ease restrictions on birth control. They want to encourage more births, because the more kids people have, the more chance they have of increasing *their* numbers. That's why you have people like that woman in Texas who killed all six of her kids – people like her realize what they are, and they try to put a stop to them but nobody *sees it!*"

"You didn't answer my question earlier," Naomi said. Now she knew she had him. His mention of Andrea Yates was the clincher. If she could now only gain his trust further, get him off guard so she could save herself and escape... "I asked you what your son did. Tell me."

Greg Oliver paused for a moment, than relaxed. He sat on the sofa next to her, no longer intent on keeping her mouth shut. "Lady, believe me, I'd love to tell you but –"

"You don't trust me," Naomi said, frowning slightly. "Look, you've got to trust me with some of this, Greg. Believe me, if I wanted you caught I would have screamed, and the way the police are canvassing this neighborhood, you and I know somebody would hear me."

His eyes narrowed. "Why do you want to know so much?"

She felt an ache in her heart as her answer yearned to burst out of her. "Because it's... well, like I said... I see... a lot of things in my practice..."

His eyes widened. All the color seemed to drain from his face. "What kind of things?"

"Two years ago one of my clients, a little girl..." she chose her words carefully. "...she killed another little girl. She was at this little girl's house playing, and...my client pushed her friend down a flight of steps. The little girl died instantly of a broken neck. The police were involved, but my client...was only five when it happened. She didn't understand! She was distraught...she said it was an accident and the performance she put on...it convinced the police and the social workers that what happened was an accident." Her voice lowered to a whisper. "But it wasn't."

"How do you know it wasn't?" Greg asked.

Naomi was silent for a moment. "It wasn't the first time she'd done it. She tried to choke another playmate once. And the little girl that was pushed down the steps? One time... my client swung a belt at her, hitting her in the face. My client wanted to kill that little girl. And... and..."

Before she totally lost it, Greg interrupted her. "My son Tony drowned his little brother." His voice was tortured, dripping with raw pain. "He drowned Marky in the bathtub. Connie had nothing to do with it! I *caught* him doing it. I... I didn't get there in time to..to save him!"

Greg almost lost it. She waited with bated breath, willing her own tears back and listened as Greg told her what he'd been through with his oldest son, Tony. "...he was always a handful but there was something just...*different* about him...it was as if he knew what we – his mother and I – were thinking. Every time we tried to discipline him or correct him in any way, he would only do something worse...it was as if he were testing us. And then we started hearing from his day care providers that they were having trouble with him. His pediatrician diagnosed him with ADD, but I knew it wasn't that. It wasn't until his day care providers told us they could no longer care for him that I started looking for more serious help. Tony was in three different day care providers and saw four different child psychologists in a five month period. When he –"

"Is that why you tried to kill him?" Naomi asked.

Greg took a deep breath. She waited for him to answer, noting out of the corner of her eye that it was now almost eleven. She had a little over four hours until her daughter, Laura, came home.

"I saw him slipping rat poison into my wife's coffee a few days ago," Greg said slowly. "I... I didn't let him know I'd seen him and I waited till he left. Then I poured the poisoned coffee down the sink and went upstairs and filled the bathtub. I was thinking about Marky and what Tony had done to him. The police originally chalked that up to an accident, you see. Marky was only a year old and Tony was only two at the time. The prosecutor wanted to press charges against Connie, but there just wasn't any evidence. Connie had been beside herself with grief – she'd never hurt the kids for any reason. She never even *spanked* them. So I was thinking of Marky when I filled the bathtub, and then I went downstairs and picked Tony up and he put up a fight. He kicked and screamed, bit my thumb. His screaming woke Connie up. By the time she pulled me away, I'd had Tony's head dunked under water for over a minute. By then I could hear the sirens and I left, I –"

She nodded, tears spilling down her face, remembering the rest of the story from the news.

Visit our forums and our blog by clicking on our Web site

www.shroudmagazine.com

went back to the hospital to finish the job," he said, his voice haunted. "I can't live knowing that I... I helped create... I helped spawn this...this creature..."

She was just about to say, I know what you mean, when there was a knock on the front door.

They froze, their bodies rigid. She held her breath, her heart lodged in her throat. Part of her thought, *this is your chance! You can scream now and they'll bust the door down...you might get hurt but at least—*

And on the heels of that: *No! Don't say anything!*

Greg Oliver gripped her upper arm with his hand. The doorbell rang and the knock sounded again, more firmly this time. Then, a voice: "Anybody home? This is the Orange County Sheriff's Department!"

They remained silent, hardly breathing. Naomi whispered to Greg, "Don't say anything. Don't even move, even if they go in the backyard. All the curtains are drawn and every door in the house is locked. They can't get in."

It seemed like an eternity, but they finally left. "They're gone," she said.

"Yeah." She felt him relax beside her.

For the first time Naomi realized her lower back was getting numb. She shifted position on the couch, her bound wrists chafing together. "My butt's getting numb."

Greg rose to his feet. "Let me untie you." He went to the kitchen and came back with a pair of scissors.

As he cut the duct tape that bound her wrists and ankles, she said, "They'll have to eventually start letting the people who live here back into the area again. Once that happens you can stay here for a few days, and then when the coast is clear I'll take you wherever you need to go."

Her bonds were untied now and she rubbed her wrists. He sat on the sofa, hands over his face. She could tell he was exhausted. "You hungry?" she asked.

"Yeah," he said. He looked at her. "I am."

Naomi stood up. "I'll make you a sandwich." She headed to the kitchen.

He followed her and she didn't even go for the handgun he'd left sitting on the counter. She opened the refrigerator and took out cold cuts, mayonnaise, mustard, and then she got a loaf of bread out. He watched as she prepared a sandwich, and then he went to the refrigerator and opened it. "Got anything to drink?"

"Help yourself." She opened the silverware drawer and pulled out a large butcher knife. He had just pulled out an ice-cold bottle of beer from the refrigerator when she sank the nine-inch blade deep into his abdomen.

His eyes flew open. His hands closed on hers as she twisted the knife in his gut. Aside from the initial spatter of blood on the linoleum kitchen floor, the wound didn't bleed much. She twisted the knife again, pushed it in even deeper, as deep as her straining muscles would allow, and the look in his eyes before he died seemed to search her face and ask, *why?*

Because I have to protect Laura, my daughter, she thought, jabbing the knife into him further, driving him to the ground. She almost fell on top of him as he tumbled to the floor and she scrambled to her feet, her palms slipping on the blood that was now spilling more fervently out of him. She stepped away, back against the kitchen counter, and watched as his feet jittered on the floor for a moment and then grew still.

She released the breath she was holding and almost collapsed. A wave of relief washed over her, threatening to break the damn. A few tears managed to trickle down her cheeks and she allowed herself to cry. *You did it, you beat him, you got him out of the way and most important, you saved Laura! You saved your daughter.*

Naomi didn't know how long she sat huddled on the kitchen floor crying, but it was the sound of the police helicopter overhead, still searching for Greg Oliver, that snapped her back to her senses. She glanced at the clock on the microwave oven. It was after one.

Somehow she was able to drag Greg's body into the garage and wrap it in an old, musty blanket from the laundry hamper. She shoved it into a storage space inside the garage, making sure it was concealed, then went back into the house. She hid the gun in the top drawer of her bedroom bureau. Then she spent an hour cleaning the kitchen floor, making sure to eliminate every drop of blood, then she peeled her own bloodied clothes off in the master bathroom and took a long, hot shower. She changed into fresh clothes placed her bloody clothes in the garbage and entered the house.

It was twelve forty-five.

She turned the TV on with the remote and, with the sound turned down, she tuned in to the local news.

For the next three hours she monitored the news and things developed quickly. Despite quickly securing the development, the police and SWAT team failed to locate Greg Oliver and concluded he'd slipped out as quickly as he'd gotten in. Door to door searches failed to turn him up, and there were no signs any of the homes were broken into. The search was now being widened and Greg's photo was being broadcast on all the local and regional news networks in the hope somebody had seen him.

At three-fifteen, she heard a key slip in the lock. She sighed in relief. "Laura!" she called out.

"Hi, Mom." She heard Laura set her backpack down on the floor near the hallway that led to the bedrooms, followed by the sound of her daughter's footsteps as she walked into the family room.

She held back her tears as she held her arms out. "Come here."

Her daughter hesitated a moment, concern flickering across her sensitive features, then she went to her mother's embrace. Naomi held her daughter, reveling in feeling her child's heartbeat, breathing in her scent. She could tell Laura sensed something was wrong. "What's wrong, mom?"

Naomi looked at her daughter and smiled, forcing back the tears. "Nothing, Laura. Everything's going to be okay."

"There were a lot of police around," Laura began, her features looking concerned. "What happened?"

"It's okay," She squeezed her daughter's hands reassuringly. "Everything's fine. The police were here, but I sent them away. It's okay now."

Laura's eyes remained on her mother, as if searching for the truth somewhere. Naomi smiled at her daughter. She never asked about her father anymore. Naomi had accidentally killed Larry one night when they were arguing about going to the police after Laura pushed the neighbor girl down the stairs of their house. Larry claimed Laura had beat the girl with a belt and burned her with cigarettes a few weeks before. He'd gone so far as to say their little girl was a monster.

Her child *wasn't* a monster! Laura was her baby, her child, and no matter what she did or who she was, Naomi was going to love her and care for her and protect her no matter what.

Naomi smiled at her daughter, fighting to keep the tears back. "Go change into some shorts," she said. "I'll get supper ready. Maybe later tonight I'll tell you everything and you can help me decide some things, okay?"

Laura smiled, all sweet dimples and child-like innocence. "Okay, mommy." Then Laura leaned forward and kissed Naomi's cheek, turned and skipped toward the hallway and her bedroom.

Naomi watched her go, a sad sense of relief overcoming her. *She may be a monster,* she thought, the loss filling her so suddenly, so overwhelmingly, *but she's all I've got.*

After collecting her strength, feeling sorry for what she'd done in killing Greg Oliver, a man she could instantly relate to because of her own situation, she rose to her feet and headed to the kitchen to prepare a light supper for two.

◇◇◇◇◇◇

J. F. Gonzalez is the author of several acclaimed novels of terror and suspense including *Clickers* (with Mark Williams), *Clickers II: The Next Wave* (with Brian Keene), *Survivor, Bully, Fetish,* and many others, as well as over sixty short stories and numerous articles.

The Haunted Wood

Tools and Toys

for the MAGICALLY MINDED

Handmade altars, wands, staves, staffs, athames, chalices, besoms, runes, ogham, boxes and more.

Rare and Unique Woods including:

Almond wood, Holly, English Yew, and Irish Bog Oak, and much more.

New England's preminent Pagan/Wiccan resource.

visit us today at:

www.hauntedwoodcrafts.com

...

Shroud 4 The Journal of Dark Fiction and Art

Dark Effigies
Artists Within the Genre

Inside the Head of Martin Blanco
Interview by Tim Deal

1. Who are some of your influences?

I have had many influences beginning with the ancient masters such as Caravaggio and Michelangelo, concerning their use of light and color. Since I started using digital techniques and doing research, I like and follow the work of Ashley Wood, Mike Bohatch, Chad Michael Ward, and many more. I like to be continuously updated on new things the artists of which I admire come out with, and also follow and research the evolution of their techniques.

2. What kind of art were you creating in your 7th grade art class?

Around 1999, I was making pencil drawings, developing a series about death and time called "Adagio." The work was exhibited in Argentina and Barcelona in 2000 and 2001.

3. What was or is your preferred media?

I always drew with graphite until 2003. I used to make large drawings, mixing pencil and ink.
From 2003 to the present, I have been working with digital, using Photoshop. The software gives me the freedom I have been looking for to be able to combine different images and textures. It also increases production speed because I don't need to wait until the paint or ink dries. Everything is easier and faster in digital.

4. Favorite 1980s teen comedy?

Revenge of the Nerds

5. Favorite 1970s horror flick?

The Exorcist and *Alien*

6. Name three things that absolutely terrify you.

Clowns. I hate them, I remember myself as a kid going to a circus (the first and last time, of course) and crying when clowns appeared. I still get a strange feeling when I see them. Darkness, too. The first thing I feel when I am in a dark place, with no lights, is that there is someone or something behind my back, staring. When I was younger, I think until I was 20 or so, I had phobia of cockroaches. I used to react the same way as women do to rats. I wasn't even able to kill them.

7. Can you give us the evolution of your current technique?

When a friend gave me an old Macintosh in 2002, I discovered Photoshop and realized the world of possibilities that it offered. I have always liked to mix different things in my drawings. But it was hard work sometimes because the paper doesn't allow you to use different materials on it. I started making pencils drawings, scanning them, and playing with texture, color, and contrast and brightness. The next step was using a pen tablet to draw directly into the computer. I had a hard time, but doing research and trying different possibilities, I learned. Regarding my image and composition, I have always been influenced and attracted to horror aesthetic, especially horror movies and comics. So I think it has been a natural development process finding my own style, my own colors and my own energy to communicate what's in my imagination.

8. Where do you find your subjects (people objects locations?)

I keep a digital camera at hand, collect images that I take as well as some taken by my friends. I prepared a large stock of images for reference.

9. Tell us two things no one knows about you...

Hmmm, secrets are secrets my friend... sorry about that

10. Where can we expect to see your work in 2009? What direction are you planning to take your art?

I am currently finishing a project with a writer friend, illustrating her poems, which will be exhibited in the Principality of Andorra in 2009.
I am making a series of 20-25 digital works called "Insane Postcards" which I think will be exhibited entirely in 2009 too; hopefully, the first part of the project (11 images) will be exhibited in Andorra. The opening was September 11th. I am also planning the release of self-published book of my work.

"Gemini" by Martin Blanco

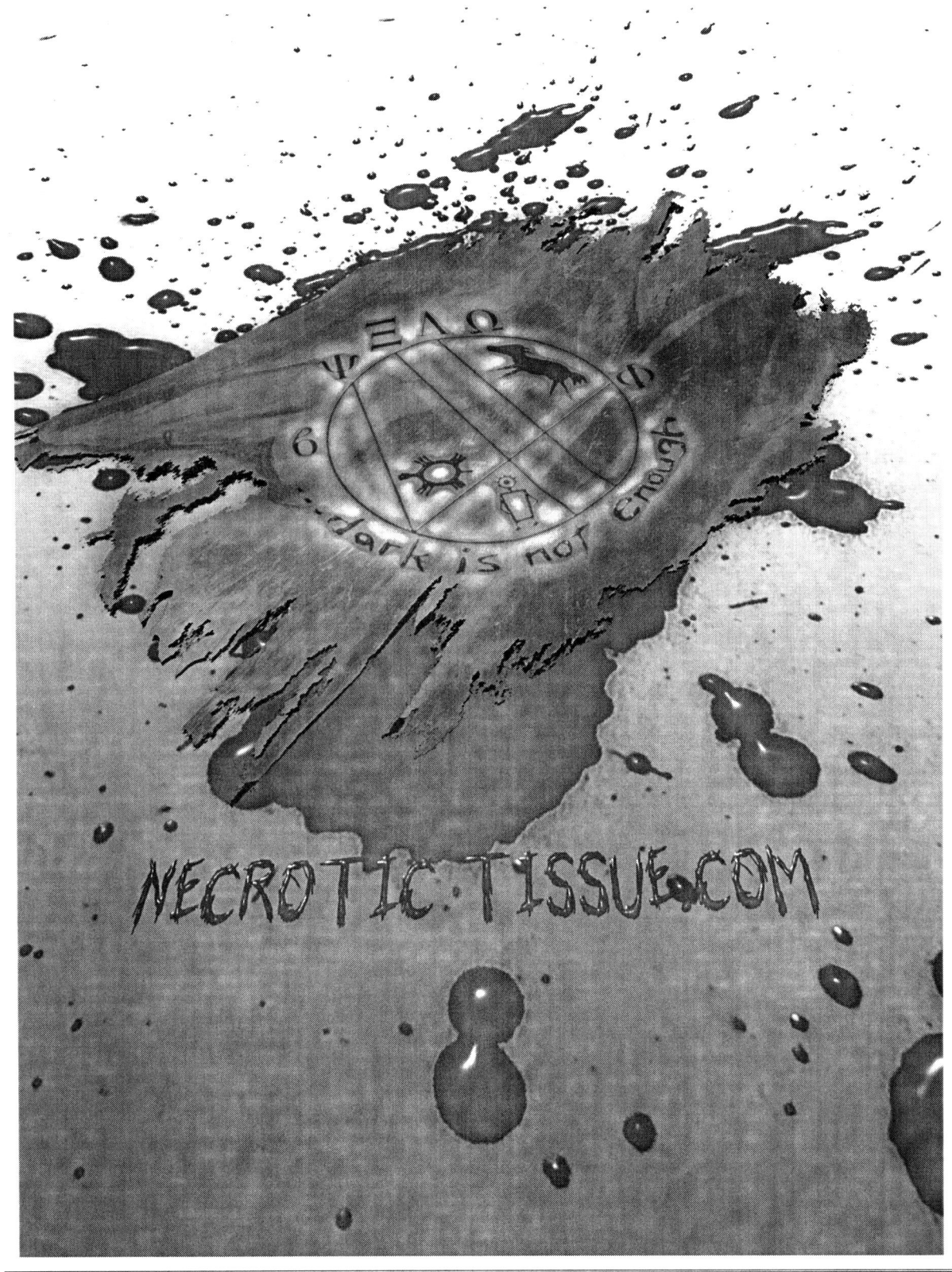

Shroud 4   The Journal of Dark Fiction and Art

Priming Pamela

Lauren Salkin

Pamela opened her eyes to a room devoid of color and contrast, a place without depth or distinction, caught in a storm of white. Lying atop a hospital gurney, she lifted her head and scanned the sheet that covered her torso. Only her pink toes were visible, wiggling freely. Something beneath the sheet restrained her arms and legs.

"Help," she screamed, but no echo followed or click, click, click of heels in response. Just silence and finality to the word "help" that seemed to vanish in a puff of sound.

Pamela leaned back against the gurney and wondered how she had landed in the middle of nothing. She remembered a world before this with a husband named John, a mother, a dead father, two friends and a nine-to-five secretarial job--a world filled with movement, harsh noises and sudden intrusions.

She closed her eyes to zip through her thoughts—-a whoosh of time: a wedding, honeymoon, memories spinning in her head like a Cup-A-Whirl ride at the amusement park. The images flew by so fast she couldn't hold onto them—-a birth, a baby's Bris, and a funeral or two.

Outside her thoughts, a gust of wind brushed her cheek. She opened her eyes to a blur of blue. A face with a surgical mask and two blue eyes hovered above the gurney. She noticed a familiar scent--Paco Raban. A lost moment she had somehow found.

She was a child again seated on her father's lap while he played the piano.

"Pamela."

"Father?" she whispered, but the memory receded into the invisible walls of endless white.

"No, Pamela. I'm Dr. Quinn. You're a very lucky lady."

"What's going on?"

"You passed out at your desk at work. We determined that the event was not organic in nature but rooted in the psychosis--a panic attack, in other words."

Pamela watched the blue material on the mask move as he spoke. His words made sense. She had blacked out before, during a piano recital in her high school auditorium. Her parents clapped with the crowd in the seats. The loud staccato sound upset her equilibrium, sent her tumbling off the bench onto the stage. But that was history, or so she had thought.

Why did she pass out today?

In the background, hushed voices chanted, "We saved you, Pamela. We saved you from yourself."

She trembled as the words repeated.

"We saved you from yourself."

"What's that?" she said, staring into the doctor's blue eyes, a stark contrast to the harshness of white.

"What's what?" the doctor asked.

"The voices."

"I'm sorry. I don't know what you're talking about."

She couldn't believe that he didn't hear them, too. Was she going mad?

"We saved you from yourself," the voices echoed.

"I-I-I don't understand."

"Of course," he nodded. "That is often the case."

"What's the case?"

"I just said, of course, Pamela. Maybe you should rest. Another doctor or two or three will be here shortly to speak with you."

"No, Doctor, uh . . ."

"Dr. Dilotta."

She shuddered. That was her maiden name. "Uh, Dr. Dilotta?"

"Pamela, I'm Dr. Quinn."

"What's going on? I know what I heard." She tried to sit up but the straps prevented movement. "Why am I strapped down?"

She waited for the eyes that did not blink, did not flutter around in the almond shaped sockets that held the answer to her question. They simply stared cold at her, then the mask moved and said, "Pamela, there are no straps."

"I know what I feel," she groaned, struggling to lift her arms and legs, but they wouldn't move.

The accusatory voices in the background grew louder. "We saved you from yourself."

"No, no, no," she shouted.

"We saved you from yourself."

Dr. Quinn approached Pamela and

placed a spectral hand on her shoulder. As he leaned over, she smelled whiskey on his breath, an odor she knew intimately from childhood—the odor that meant anger, and fear, and ducking from stuff thrown at her. The odor that permeated from her father's glass eventually turned his liver into a bloated pouch of flesh.

A foul liquid peaked hot in Pamela's throat, before slipping back down. "I want my husband," she demanded, her bottom lip quivering. The doctor poked her shoulder. "No husband for you. You were bad. Tsk, Tsk."

"What?" she screamed.

"They said that you might not want to be touched."

"You jabbed me, goddamn it."

"Poor child cannot tell the difference between a jab and a touch."

"That's not true." Her father gently pressed his fingers against her lips at bedtime and whispered, "Shhhhh, no more talking. Go to sleep."

He only jabbed her during piano lessons and said, "Practice, my little girl, practice, and one day you will be like the others."

But she didn't want to be like the others. They played dead people's music. She liked things that were alive, like the melodies in her head. She wanted to write songs.

Pamela remembered working on a song before the computer monitor blurred and she awakened in a world of white. She couldn't think of the tune now. Though, she could recall the feeling of discovery, and passion, and burst of musical notes that randomly sequenced into a song. But here in the white place, there were no colors, or songs, or sensations, other than fear, confusion and anger.

John understood her and listened to her sequenced notes, except when he was lost in one of his sci-fi shows. A wave of his hand signaled her to leave the room.

Pamela shook her head and dismissed the shadows that obscured the colors in her memory, focusing instead on the doctor's blue surgical mask.

He winked, then with a turn of his head, he was gone without a word or sound. Only the scent of whiskey and Paco Raban remained.

Another attempt to free herself proved useless. Though her toes, those lovely pink toes continued to wiggle. She watched them for a while. Until a set of eyes wrapped in white approached. How strange the eyes looked. Circles with brown blotches in the center floated towards her.

When the eyes hovered by her side, Pamela detected another familiar scent, lemon bath powder, the odor that belonged to her mother. Day after day Pamela breathed in the acrid citrus fumes, while her mother plodded around the house in a pink terrycloth bathrobe, muttering, "You could have been better than this."

"Mother?" she croaked. The lemon scent always caught in her throat. "Water."

The eyes stared at her as accusingly as her mother used to do. "So, what will it be?" they demanded.

"Water." Pamela coughed.

A hiss of sound and a cup appeared in front of her. She lifted her head and drank from it. After several gulps, the cup disappeared. She lay back on the gurney.

"Let's see," said the eyes, with lips that had a smear of red around them.

"It's obvious," interjected another set of eyes and lips that drifted toward her. The new lips glistened with a shade of pink.

There was nothing distinct about the two faces. A comic book artist could have drawn them. They had no depth and no body to anchor them. They were just two sets of eyes, a nose and mouth, with hair pulled back in a cap.

"You passed out," said the red lips.

Pink lips chimed in. "Yes, you passed out at your desk."

"That's bad," said Red. "You need to purge yourself of toxins to help maintain your mental balance."

"To save you from yourself," they said in unison with the voices in the background.

"Stop this. Right now," Pamela yelled. "I'm sick and tired of hearing that I need to be saved."

Red prodded Pamela with an index finger. "I didn't say anything like that."

Pink agreed.

"I know what I heard."

"Do you?" responded Red. "I think you are suffering from a deep psychosis. You hear melodies in your head. Do you not?"

"How do you know?"

Red's voice raised an octave--"I'm your mother. I know everything."--Then sank to alto. "They found music notes scribbled on the memo you were typing."

"You're not my mother. Though, you smell like her."

Red and Pink exchanged glances.

"Ah, now we are getting somewhere."

"But I'm not. I'm not getting anywhere," said Pamela and watched another quick eye exchange between Red and Pink.

"I want to call my husband."

"John told us you would say that," mocked Red.

"What? When?"

"An hour or two or three ago.

He's here, waiting for you in the receiving area. He believes that a fundamental change in your character is long overdue."

"No. You're lying. He'd rescue me if he knew I was here. He's home in his basement office writing a business proposal."

Loud, resounding laughter.

Pink caught her breath, said, "We didn't find him in the basement."

More laughter.

"John. I'm here," screamed Pamela. "Help!" She tried to rock the gurney, but it wouldn't budge. "Get me out of here!"

"We can't," said Red.

"Why? Why can't you?"

"As long as you see color toxins in your mind, you have to stay."

"We have to save you from yourself."

"You need to be like the others."

"You have to sit in your chair with your hands folded on the desk."

Pamela smelled chalk and crayons.

"Like all the other children," Pink said.

"I don't want to be like the other children."

"If you don't want to pass out anymore, you must be."

"Why do I pass out?"

"You have too many colorful thoughts bouncing around in your brain disturbing your equilibrium."

With that, they ripped the sheet off her. She groaned. Black and white veins crisscrossed beneath the translucent skin on her legs. Her toes were the only part of her still pink, the only part she could move. An intravenous tube protruded from her thigh, extended down her leg to her ankle, and slipped through a hole in the gurney.

"Get it off," screamed Pamela, as the pink in her toes faded to gray.

"You're almost done," said Red.

"When your toes become black and white, the transition will be complete. Then you can go."

Pamela stared at Red and Pink. Their lips started losing color. "Your lips have no color," whispered Pamela.

"A very good sign," they answered in unison.

"No, no. Your lips!"

"Your lips are our lips," they said.

"I don't understand. Oh, God. Why do this to me?"

The voices in the background and the lips chanted, "To save you."

"From who?"

"From yourself."

With every echo of their words, the gray in the lips and the pink of her toes inched darker until the change was complete.

Pamela stared at her black and white toes and willed them to move. Nothing happened. Not even a twitch. She looked at the lips with tears in her eyes. "Who will save me from you?"

They just laughed. And the word "Done" resounded throughout the periphery of white. The lips smiled and drifted away.

"Remember, Pamela," they said. "In the other world, everyone sees black and white. Now you will fit right in. Fit right in."

Before the lips disappeared, Pamela shouted after them one last time, but it was too late. Her white surroundings rushed away, taking the air with it. Around her, white morphed to gray, then to black. Pamela gasped, choking, struggling to breathe. In darkness, she groped for a lifeline. Nothing to hold to but emptiness. Nothing to touch, but to feel--pain.

Pamela grabbed her thigh. Slowly, her focus sharpened from a blur of gray. She sat at her workstation facing a black desk and white computer monitor. The clock in the upper, right corner of the screen flashed 4:20 p.m. Pamela frowned. The last thing she remembered was waiting for someone to meet her. She checked the calendar and saw the notation: John, 12:30 lunch. She drew a blank. Where had the day gone? She rubbed her leg.

Without a warning of approaching footsteps, a voice blasted her from behind. "How are you feeling?"

Pamela swiveled in her chair.

Mr. Paulson had poked his head inside her cubicle. His lips curled into a thin smile. "Ah. He brought you back all fixed up."

For a moment she thought, "Who brought me back from where?" But, instead, she answered, "Much better, Mr. Paulson."

"Good," he replied with a quick swipe of tongue across his lower lip. "Now finish typing that memo and enjoy it."

Pamela stared at the short, stocky man, his black hair peppered with gray. For some reason, he didn't offend her today.

"Oh, by the way," he added. "Your husband is also thrilled you're better. He told me so when he dropped you off."

Again, the questions that crowded her mind skulked away like forgotten children.

Pamela smiled at Mr. Paulson, comforted by her colorless thoughts. What a sweet man.

After he slipped from view, she whirled around to her desk, where the draft of a memo lay. Lines of music notes stretched across the top of the page. She gazed at the notes, wondering why they were there.

She dismissed the distraction and assumed the position in front of the computer monitor. With fingers curved over the keyboard, she poked at the black keys with white letters, a soothing, rhythmic click-click-click. A nice repetitious motion helped clear her mind of colorful toxins.

◇◇◇◇◇

Lauren Salkin works an Advertising Production Manager for a parenting magazine. During Lauren's free time, she writes humorous essays and dark short stories. Lauren's publishing credits include ByLine Magazine, The Front Porch Syndicate, The Ridgefield Press, and the Connecticut Authors & Publishers Association Newsletter.

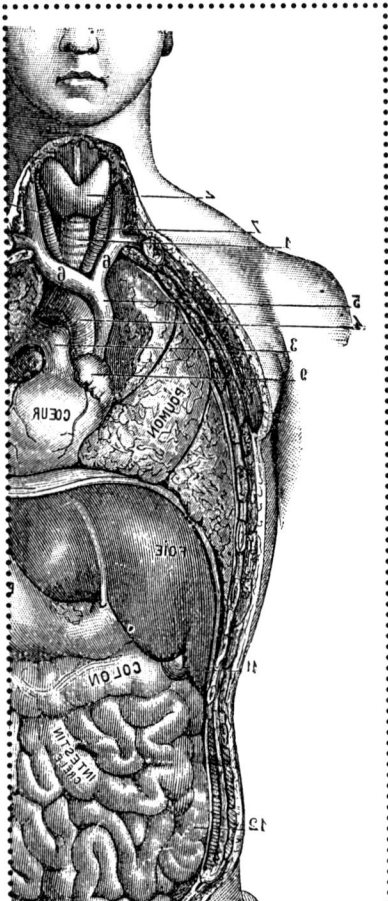

Bram Stoker Award Finalist and Author of *Dead Souls*

MICHAEL LAIMO

FIRES RISING

"Laimo can stand proud next to Clive Barker and Stephen King."
—*The Horror Review*

AVAILABLE NOW!
WWW.LAIMO.COM
WWW.AMAZON.COM

GRIMOIRES AND TOMES

Book Reviews

THE DARKEST EVENING OF THE YEAR, Dean Koontz

Review by I.E. Lester

Amy Redwing, a foundling raised by nuns, runs a dog rescue centre called The Golden Heart. She is dedicated to her mission, willing to risk herself physically and financially to help Golden Retrievers in danger.

When she and her boyfriend Brian rescue Nickie, they get more than just a dog. For one thing, she also rescues the family who owns Nickie at the time, calling 911 on the violent husband and father. However, there is something special about Nickie.

The relationship between Amy and Brian is fragile and very chaste. Both have immense emotional baggage. In addition to the mental, these pasts are about to return to haunt them in a very physical sense.

Brian's ex-wife is self-centred, spiteful, and cruel. She blames their handicapped daughter for her relationship issues and does not hesitate in making the girl suffer for it. She doesn't want the girl but is not about to let Brian have her without making him pay.

Amy's ex- is also back. And he, too, is unwilling to let things lie. Amy thought that when she left him, she would be free of his abuse and domination. However, his need to control has not ended, and although he does not want her back, he doesn't want her to be happy without him. Therefore, he hires a mercenary to stalk her, burgle her home, and generally, make her life unpleasant.

This book is crammed with content. We have a number of rescue stories - both of dogs and people. We have a moral diatribe on the treatment of dogs in breeding centres, domestic violence, and child abuse, a hired killer called Bookworm who uses literary aliases - mostly from Kurt Vonnegut novels - vengeful ex-partners, a supernatural undertone, and a love story all wrapped up in one book.

That it isn't completely confusing can only be a credit to Dean Koontz. He manages to weave the strands into a whole, but at a cost. The elements jar against each other somewhat and some of the joins feel strained. It results in the book being less satisfying than some of his earlier novels.

It is entertaining though - *The Darkest Evening of the Year* contains much of the storytelling ability that has seen Koontz's name regularly top bestseller lists since the 1980s. But it doesn't gel fully - the narrative flow actually feels choppy at times. But even below his best, Koontz is still worth reading.

Available on Amazon.com for

Shroud 4   The Journal of Dark Fiction and Art

$7.99

QUEEN OF BLOOD, Bryan Smith

Review by I.E. Lester

If you've read Brian Smith's "House of Blood," you will have a head start on this world and the author's general style. Fortunately, though, this is not a requirement to reading "Queen of Blood." Suffice it to say, 2004's "House of Blood" concerned a house of death ruled over by a powerful, supernatural, and very twisted master - who was overthrown.

Following the death of the master, his servant, Ms. Wickman, is intent on creating her own house of death, gore, pain, and suffering. The problem for her, though, is that she's not the only one to have this idea.

A number of the survivors of the first book have been tainted by their proximity to the Death Gods and are now very much on their own path to true evil - a path laced with orgies, torture, mutilations, and blood pouring out of pretty much everywhere. This really isn't subtle.

What you are treated to here is over three hundred pages of mayhem and violence, sacrifice and bloodletting, all wrapped up in an exceptionally dark mythology.

The action is near relentless, and very, bloodily graphic. Smith has no hesitation when it comes to ripping flesh and sinews, smashing bone and popping eyeballs. His "evils" (the Death Gods) are absolute, pure, and without redeeming features. His "goods," well that isn't an easy thing to comment upon - there really aren't any.

The only thing Bryan Smith leaves out of this book is a truly likeable, good person - the character who stands out from the start as the survivor. Those characters that are not pure evil are selfish; nobility just doesn't take feature in this book. Almost anyone could die in this book, and from the start, you feel almost everyone will. It keeps you guessing. However, it does also distance you, making it a good deal harder for the reader to become involved in the story.

Another down point has to be the plot. You wouldn't exactly call it detailed. In fact, barring the slight side plot of a survivalist colony out in the wilds, the plot is a one-premise pony. It's a simple idea on which the author has tacked as many splatterfest scenes as he could until he's run out of body parts to hack off or squash into pulp.

This is the novel for fans of slash-horror movies. It reads like a compilation of all the goriest bits from any ten other horror novels - fine if you like gore overload but lightweight in terms of drama.

Available on Amazon.com for $6.57

INSTITUTIONAL MEMORY, Gary Frank

Review by I.E. Lester

Life at Osprey Publishing is dull, a monotonous nine-to-five existence in a depressing, unloved, and uncared for office block called the *Howard Phillips* building. Things change, and for the worse, when Sharon Walters is taken prisoner by the building.

Her colleagues don't initially suspect anything supernatural - her friends worry Sharon might have been kidnapped. But their opinions soon change as the building is not satisfied with just one victim and it soon begins to attack more of the workforce.

Gary Frank has created his own twisted, gory version of Sick Building Syndrome. This isn't about health hazards such as headaches, dry coughs, nausea or fatigue often associated with poor heated and ventilated ageing buildings. Frank's version of a sick building is closer to more a possess building. In this office you are more likely to be attacked by cables descending from the ceiling intent on a bit of demonic hack and slay.

There doesn't seem to be a stable, happy person in this entire book. Even given the horror element things are going right for any of the characters. Mousy Marcy is a timid thing, scared of men (understandably given her last relationship), Goth-chick Bettie self-harms, and Jon is trapped in a failing marriage, forced into a job he doesn't want by a controlling and unfaithful wife.

Given time enough they are likely to destroy themselves, without the building even bothering to try. But the author has managed to make the three main characters just likeable enough so that you, the reader, will invest in them and root for them.

This book is fairly original; there aren't all that many books about possessed office blocks. And despite some clumsy scene setting early in the book it is well paced, with just enough action spread throughout the book to keep up the interest without it being an endless gore-fest.

Frank has also written his "bad-guy" well. The entity controlling the building is not perfect. Not everyone it attacks is captured. Although clearly powerful and malevolent this evil isn't seemingly all-powerful.

Too often in horror, the big bad is too big, resulting in conclusions that seem too handy - the Achilles Heel, plucked as though from the ether at the last minute, that wins the day for the good guys in an unsatisfactory manner. Plot manipulation. However, here you believe the trio of Jon, Bettie and Marcy could defeat the building.

And it's evident the author is a true horror fan - the novel is set in the *Howard Phillips* building in a reverential nod of the head to one of the greats. The cables falling from ceiling panels and grasping for anyone within reach feels very much like a mechanised H.P. Lovecraft tale.

This is a satisfying horror. Gary Frank will be a name to look for in the years to come.

Available on Amazon.com for $7.95

∞∞∞∞∞∞∞∞∞∞∞∞∞∞∞∞

RAVENOUS, Ray Garton
Review by I.E. Lester

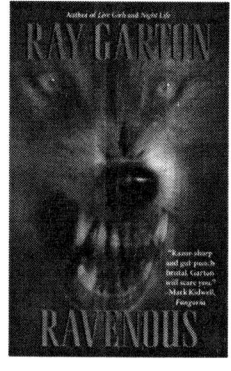

Emily Crane is attacked and raped on her way back from a weight-watchers class. She fights back, however, stabbing her rapist through the eye with a discarded corkscrew.

Sheriff Arlin Hurley believes that Emily has killed the serial attacker dubbed "The Pine County Rapist". His hopes don't last as the corpse revives and walks from the morgue, savagely killing one of Hurley's deputies. Soon, more people turn up dead and mutilated.

After a further set of murders, Daniel Fargo approaches Hurley with a warning - his town is infested with werewolves, that conventional policing methods will not succeed, and that they only have a limited time before the spread of the infection becomes unstoppable.

In some ways, this is just a stereotypical werewolf story. However, Garton's plot involving lycanthropy as a sexually transmitted disease is a good twist, but not a major change. Werewolves are still simply infected humans who change into monsters and eat people, and the main method to defeat them is still silver.

But, here a lack of originality is not a downer. As with vampire stories, the werewolf myth is a part of culture. Maintaining the status quo in a vampire or werewolf tale is not as dangerous as introducing variations on the theme and mythos. Therefore, we must judge Garton's story on its own merits as a story.

The pacing is excellent, getting off to a flying start with a series of attacks in the opening pages, before taking a breath to add some character-development, then picking the pace up again, building to the climax. Garton's novel grabs your attention from the off, commits you fully by making the people real, and then goes for the throat (no pun intended) with an all-action ending.

Taking that pause to build a cast would not have worked if the characters had not been worth developing. Given this structure, creating second rate stereotypes would have been a disaster.

Garton does not fail us though.

His cast is diverse - a worldly wise sheriff, a teenager with a crush on his neighbour, a middle-aged couple with marital problems, an abusive husband and his submissive wife and a highly-sexed woman who seems to be having an affair with half the town's men.

There are a couple of great elements to this book. When the sheriff and his deputies are told of the existence of werewolves, their level of scepticism is perfect. After all, if someone came up to you in the street (as Fargo does to Hurley) and tells you that monsters are real, your first thought would be to doubt their sanity. But their disbelief is not everlasting; no one stubbornly clings to denial in the face of the grisly evidence.

Garton plays up the feeling of the unexpected. In many horror novels, readers can predict who are the survivors virtually from page one. Not so here - no one is guaranteed to get out alive and that adds a great deal of suspense. Ray Garton's *Ravenous* is a wonderful read - great fun!

Available on Amazon.com for $7.99

Shroud is interested in reviewing published works of dark speculative fiction.

Please send advance review copies at least one month before publication date, accompanied by appropriate press materials. Shroud is also available for jacket blurbs provided that the content is sent well-enough in advance.

Other books can be sent at any time with the understanding that we cannot guarantee that we will review everything and review materials cannot be returned. Sorry!

Send review materials (books, DVDs, Games, CDs) to:

**Shroud Publishing
121 Mason Rd.
Milton, NH 03851**

Questions? editor@shroudmagazine.com

Windows to the Soul
Film and DVD Reviews

Peter Medak's, *The Changeling*
Marie O'Regan

Strangely for a film that made such an impression on me, certain things escape my memory, such as where I saw it or who with. Two images though, stand out clearly in my mind – a wheelchair, and a wet rubber ball. That and the sensation of the hairs at the back of my neck prickling.

The Changeling was released in 1980, starring George C Scott and Trish van Devere, and it was directed by Peter Medak, known most recently for the series *Carnivàle*, as well as films such as *Pontiac Moon* and *Romeo Is Bleeding*. Medak has told the story of how – on reading the script upstairs in his bedroom – he was so scared he couldn't move.

A ghost story, *The Changeling* is reminiscent of *Audrey Rose* (1977) and *Don't Look Now* (1973) in its main theme: a child haunting the living and a father figure seeking the truth. The difference lies in the murder mystery irrevocably woven through it. Scott plays John Russell, a composer and piano teacher who – after losing his family in a car accident – moves to Seattle, renting a house from the historical society. The house is haunted, setting the scene for a truly frightening film.

Medak viewed *The Changeling* as a 'Hitchcockian ghost story' and wanted to create that same air of mystery and suspense. Rick Wilkins' swirling score underpins this admirably, and the subdued cinematography sustains the mystery by making it difficult for us to see who, or what, is coming into shot.

Medak used the exterior of a huge, gothic building he found on an island off the coast of Vancouver as a 'façade', but the interior was a vast, four storey composite set that was constructed especially so that Medak had more space to employ tracking shots (as in *The Shining*, which came out the same year). The use of the newly designed 'Steadicam' helped greatly in this. Medak used either tracking shots, or shots edited together to appear as such, to draw us along with the characters on their travels – in some scenes the tracks were painted to appear like the carpets so that we didn't see them, or the POV was above floor-level for the same reason. The effect is that of a journey, with the viewer being literally drawn into, and along with, the narrative. Doorways abound in this film, both actual - which we follow the camera through – and metaphoric, the doorway between life and death, which both Russell and the ghost are seeking to open, although from opposite sides and for different reasons. We are aware from the beginning that Russell is being watched, through the use of 'high shots', where the camera pans upwards at the end of each shot, to show us the view from above, the ghost's POV.

Water also plays a dominant role in the film, with taps dripping, being left on – he is woken each morning by a booming sound that appears to come from the pipes, and is eventually drawn by the sound of water to a bathroom in the attic, where he sees a vision of a drowned boy in the tub. Next to the bathroom, Russell discovers a boarded over door. Medak employs the 'rule of three' here – the padlock breaks when he hits it for the third time with the hammer (accompanied by the booming sound that has woken him each day) and the door opens when he is about to hit it with his shoulder for the third time. It's a child's room, and Russell finds a wheelchair (the scene later in the film where the wheelchair chases a terrified Trish van Devere out of the house is both scary and unintentionally funny – certainly one you remember), and a music box that plays the tune he thought he had just composed. From this point on the ghost 'comes out to play', even taking his dead daughter's ball to play with. When it bounces down the stairs towards him, Russell drops it into a nearby river, only to have the now wet ball bounce down the stairs to land at his feet when he returns home

The Changeling is the tale of a crippled child murdered by his father so that a healthy, and therefore more suitable, heir can be substituted – the eponymous changeling (played to great effect by Melvyn Douglas, in one of his last roles, as Senator Joseph Carmichael). His denial when confronted is supremely touching - he is furious, denying it all: "My father was not a murderer. No one in this world could say that!" But someone not in this world has said it – the real Joseph.

If I go into too much more detail here it'll spoil the film for those who haven't seen it yet. Suffice to say that certain scenes retain the power to scare even after seeing them several times. The one that sticks out is the séance organised by Russell to seek the truth of who, or what, is attempting to communicate with him. Medak visited a number of séances to establish the correct tone for the scene, and it shows – this is one of the most chilling parts of the entire film. It also establishes the ghost as a character in his own right. When Russell plays the audiotape back later, he hears the child's voice and we segue into a flashback to the boy's death. The child, a cripple, is held underwater by his father till he drowns. The booming sound we've heard throughout the film is revealed to be the sound the child's arm makes as he bangs against the side of the metal tub. Truly disturbing, it is doubtful whether the scene would today get past the censors in its entirety. The scene – a precursor to films such as White Noise in its use of EVP, or Electric Voice Phenomena – where Scott replays the tape alone, and we hear the boy's voice: *"Joseph ... my room ... can't walk ... my father ... my room ... the well ... Sacred Heart ... my medal ... father ... don't ... help ... help ... my body ... ranch ... the well...my name ... Joseph Carmichael ..."* manages to be scary and plaintive simultaneously. No mean feat.

A more modern horror film that contains a nod to *The Changeling* is *The Ring*, with its scene of a body's discovery in a well being an almost direct remake of one in *The Changeling*, testament to the film's enduring power to stay in the memory long after you've seen it.

There have been films that scared me more, *The Exorcist*, *The Uninvited*, *The Birds* – but *The Changeling* stood out in a way the others didn't, and a large part of that was its quietness, the way it built its atmosphere so slowly that you almost didn't notice until you were immersed in the tale – and that stays with you far longer than something that relies on gore to inspire fear.

◇◇◇◇◇◇◇◇

Marie O'Regan, is a writer and freelance journalist, writing for magazines such as Fortean Times, Writing Magazine, Writers' Forum, Dreamwatch, Death Ray, Dark Side, Rue Morgue, Red Scream and Hub, among others. Marie is a regular contributor to Shroud.

THE BULB

By ERNESTO BURDEN

Martha and the kids, Jamie and Ruth, had been in the house in Manchester for almost two months when the thing with Jamie's hand happened. It was mid-October. James, Jamie and Ruth's dad, had just found an apartment in Buffalo. He'd called that morning to say hello to the kids. Ruth had been excited, spilling over with a four-year-old's delighted gabble of silly stories, half-real, half-imagined, streams of words said for the delight in saying them. Jamie had refused to come to the phone. He was six. He understood what was happening. That Daddy was not just on a business trip or a fishing vacation. Daddy was not going to live with them anymore. Jamie had not forgiven his parents. They had not forgiven each other.

"Get in here and say hello to your father," Martha had hissed from the kitchen, covering the mouthpiece with her hand so James wouldn't hear. "You come here right now."

"Why do you care?" Jamie demanded. He stood in the living room, body leaned toward her as though he longed to run to her, to his father, to be close to them, but his face was defiant. "You don't want me to talk to daddy. You made him leave."

"I didn't make him leave," she said, though that wasn't exactly the truth. Her voice was rising and she could hear James in the earpiece.

"Just forget it," he was saying. "If he's upset he…"

"You come in here right now," she'd said, voice suddenly low.

She and Jamie glared at each other. The moment stretched, like elastic growing tenser and tighter even as it lengthened.

"I won't," Jamie said and bolted past her out the kitchen door. She ignored whatever James was saying, his voice an insignificant buzzing from the phone's earpiece. She pressed the headset against her forehead and tried to ignore the hot tears on her cheeks, to ignore the blood rushing in her ears, to ignore the dark sorrow that seemed to be expanding in her chest like a balloon, crushing her lungs so she couldn't breathe.

That afternoon she was planting bulbs, the black balloon still swollen in her chest, her head replaying the morning's conversation again and again. James and Jamie. Damn them both. She'd come back out of the house about ten minutes before, after cleaning a little cut in her finger – an old piece of broken glass buried in the yard by the fence had punched right through her cloth gardening glove while she'd picked rocks from a fresh hole. Pricked her just enough to make her bleed a few swollen crimson drops into the hole she'd been digging. She'd thought it would have been worse, but by the time she washed her hands with soap in the bathroom, the cut had nearly closed.

It had been cool all day and now Martha thought she could begin to see puffs of her own breath in the air. There was a smell of wood smoke – one of the neighbors had a fire. She scanned the rooftops and found one of the neatly capped chimneys adorned with a plume of picturesque white smoke. The sun was dipping below the tops of the trees that filled the ragged, stony gully that fell away on the north side of the patchy yard, toward the Piscatquog River, where it rippled through the city like a smooth band of muscle, deceptively gentle, unexpectedly strong. Jamie had taken to playing in the gully, following the little paths that led down the embankment. Martha had forbidden him to climb the other side and then follow the paths down the hill to the riverside.

She could hear him as he played, as his sneakers crunched the duff's dry leaves and skeleton-brittle twigs. When she heard him cry out, she thought it was part of the play. She looked up when she heard him running and saw him burst from the trees. Ruth, on the swing set, stared at her brother open-mouthed, eyes shocked wide. Jamie's hand was pouring blood.

Martha didn't have time to stand. Her son had rocketed across the lawn and was flinging himself against her, sobbing and shaking, holding the wrist of his injured hand, pulling it in against himself protectively. They knelt there, above the hole where she had just dropped a tulip bulb. His wide gray-green eyes met hers; she wanted to weep herself at the fear and shock she saw there. He held her gaze then dropped his eyes to his hand. He opened his clenched fingers.

Blood spurted from a deep gash across the palm that ran nearly up to his wrist. At first she thought his wrist was cut. There seemed to be so much blood – it had to be an artery. The blood roared from his hand, soaking both their shirts, their pants, the raw hole in the earth where she had planted the tulip bulb, soaking the bulb itself. As her eyes followed the shower of blood down, she was horrified to see it pooling, literally dammit, pooling in that hole. So much blood. And at the center of the pool, the tiny bulb, making her think, suddenly and grotesquely, of a tiny, bloody fetus ejected and dropped unceremoniously into an anonymous grave.

"What happened?" she demanded. "What happened, oh, baby, what happened?"

She shook him when he didn't answer; just stared at her with his jaw hanging open, slack, like when he walked in his sleep. His eyes goggled into hers, then through her, out the back of her head and into places she couldn't see.

Jamie," she said, her voice rising, and she heard anger along with the fear, "snap out of it and tell me what the hell happened. What happened out there?" She shook him again, harder this time. It never would have occurred to her to ask, "Who did this to you?" Never in a million years.

His eyes shifted, refocusing, and he seemed to be looking at her again, her own little boy who loved her so much he still cried to be away from her for too long. Who could not spend the night away, even with James, without melting down into hysterics in the middle of the night.

"It was the old lady," he said slowly, as though his mouth were thawing out. "The little old lady. With the scissors." Then he burst into tears again and the blood seemed to erupt again from his hand and she pulled him close, pressed her own hands around his trying to apply enough pressure to slow the geyser.

She couldn't have said how it was

possible, later, that with her six-year-old son seemingly bleeding to death in her arms, a crazy woman stalking the woods behind her home, her daughter wailing in fear on the swing set, she'd taken the time, however brief, to kick the dirt back over the bulb, to hide the tiny, naked horror in the hole. But her last memory of the spot was not of a hole at all, but of a mound. She didn't think about it until the following spring.

The police came, but they didn't find anyone behind the house. No footprints, other than Jamie's, no scissors, no knife. Jamie had bled a great deal as he fled the woods, and there was blood on sharp rocks, on jutting, splintered branches, on a tangle of old barbed wire that had once been a fence and had been grown around by one of the twisted tree trunks.

"He likely cut it on something," one of the officers told her. "A boy that age gets scared and bolts and maybe doesn't remember things exactly the way they happened. Maybe he saw a shadow, a stump that reminded him of a little old woman. It's dark in the woods, and things aren't always what they look like. "

"That's not true," she'd told him. The officer was young, with a lean jaw and probing, sympathetic eyes. He was the picture of understanding, except Martha couldn't help thinking of the word caricature instead of the word picture. He nodded too perfectly as she spoke. His lips parted just the right amount while he seemed to consider what she was saying. He answered too solemnly.

"I don't want to seem disrespectful," he told her. "A mother knows her children and how they'll react and behave better than I possibly could. But I've gotta tell you, I've responded to more than one call following an injury to a young boy like your son, and heard more than one story that's a little ... well, beyond belief. Sometimes even when the parents were right there to see the whole thing happen." He frowned as if to suggest that perhaps she should have been right there to see it. I couldn't see him, she thought, but I could hear him. He's only six. I never would have left him alone alone.

She nodded, almost without realizing she was doing it. The young policeman seemed encouraged. His voice changed somehow, his words stretched out and his pronunciation grew more precise. He began to recite.

"Like I said, lots of boys tell stories like this one; have been for fifty

---

Shroud 4   The Journal of Dark Fiction and Art

years, a hundred years around here. This old woman? Local lore. It's just a combination of factors coming into focus – the wild imagination boys have, their unwillingness to admit when they get scared at shadows, the way they boys talk to each other – at school, on the playground. The story gets passed around, and even if it's done unconsciously, ends up substituted for a more prosaic reality."

She nodded again, then frowned. A more prosaic reality. Sure.

"We haven't lived here that long," she said. "I don't know where Jamie would have heard this story... And isn't it just as likely that if all these different boys, from different homes and different times even, are telling the same story, then that's an argument for it being true instead of something each boy came up with on his own to explain away something he was scared of and didn't understand?"

He smiled gently. "Ma'am," he said, "let it go. Trust me. I told that story once when I was a boy. And in the end, I was better for it. And so were my parents."

She nodded again. His smile was warm, charming, compelling. His eyes were as compassionate – and beautiful, she couldn't help thinking – as she'd ever encountered. But she'd think about what he said, later. It was a strange thing for a policeman to say, and a strange way for him to say it.

Time passed and things got better some days, worse others. James called every other day from Buffalo. Ruth grew bored talking to him. Jamie began to miss him. Said he wished his father would call more often. Spent a half an hour on the phone with him some nights. The snow fell hard and thick that winter, global warming her ass, she thought, and they had fires in the fireplace and Jamie and Ruth lay on their bellies, chins cupped in their hands, watching the flames dance while the wind moaned outside and Martha hunted the Web for leads on photos to license of Sub-Saharan African wildlife for a National Geographic freelance gig. The job ended when the book went to the printer and things got tight for a little while as they lived on the money James sent. It wasn't alimony – they were separated, not divorced, though that was coming soon enough, she hoped. But he was good about the money. Good about calling to talk to Jamie and Ruth. Good about being a provider and trying to be a father, even that distance. It was too bad he'd been such a shit husband.

One night in early spring, Ruth woke up screaming. She and Jamie shared a room. When Martha finally calmed her down enough so she could speak, Ruth said she'd seen a face outside of Jamie's window.

"It was like a little old woman," Ruth said. "Except all flat and lumpy, like a potato." Jamie never even woke up, but in the morning he was out of sorts, grumpy and a little dazed. Martha felt lonely that day. Lonelier than she had in the ten months since James had moved out.

"I'm sorry," he'd said. It had been May, and the sun had been shining in the bluest sky she'd ever seen. The trees were flush with new green leaves and there was a yellow dusting of pollen on the cars in the driveway. James was standing at the door, wearing a worn-looking pair of brown trousers and a green T-shirt bearing a picture of a monkey with a samurai sword in its paw. The T-shirt read, "Teenage Mutant Ninja Code Monkeys." With his sandy hair and slight build, thick black rimmed glasses, he looked almost as he had when they were in college. That had been almost fifteen years ago. He had with a ratty duffel bag in one hand. She could see a rectangular shape outlined in the cheap fabric. Picture frame. She guessed it was the kids. "I have to go," he said.

"I understand," she'd said. She'd wanted to beg, to fall down on her damn knees and wrap her arms around his legs and beg. Or hit him in the head with a heavy object – maybe the base of the brass lamp from the piano. Instead she'd affected a tone of casual disinterest. She had no idea why. Hated the way her voice sounded in her head.

"You have to do what you have to do. I know you must feel hurt."

He'd stared at her then, puzzled; shook his head.

"Hurt?" he asked. Then he turned his back on her. "I don't think that's the word I'd have picked."

"What, then?" she'd asked, wishing she hadn't even as the words sailed into the warm spring air.

"You killed me," he said. Then he stepped back, onto the porch, and the screen door swung shut. He turned, without looking back, and got into his car, an old blue Civic with rust on the wheel wells. He was proud of that car – proud of the fiscal discipline, the environmental balance driving a car for 300,000 miles indicated. She thought it was a good symbol of his underlying madness.

When he slid into the driver's seat, she saw that he was crying. She'd turned back into the house then, and saw Jamie at the window, watching his father drive away. Jamie looked at her and then back out the window.

By the time May finally ended up on the front page of the calendar again, the tulips were up. All except one of them. Ruth went outside and stood staring at the spot – a brown dirt mound where no tulip – or grass or weeds even – had grown. It was bare, but not, she thought, sterile. There was something fecund about it; a hidden potential, a frightening kinetic energy buried there. The fierce power of blood, boiling beneath the earth; Jamie's blood.

She shuddered. These were not good thoughts for her to be thinking. Not when things had begun to seem a little good again. A little normal, finally.

Jamie banged out of the back door, Ruth at his heels, long black hair flowing out behind her. Martha marveled at how long her legs had gotten, how her face had lost so much of its chubby little girl look over the winter. Now her high, broad cheekbones made Martha think of elves, or pixies – beautiful and dark and a bit dangerous. And Jamie on the other hand – once long and lean and fair, now seeming skinny, almost sickly. He was wasting away.

"Are we going?" Jamie called. He ran to the swings on stick legs, launched himself, on his belly, into a wildly arcing flight, legs kicking as he swung back and forth. Ruth came to Martha and put her arms around Martha's knees. The little girl looked at the mound, curiously, then said: "That's where she stands."

"Who, sweetie?" Martha asked.

"The little mother," Ruth said. "The one who comes at night. She looks up at our window. She is waiting for her baby. She wants to be a friend."

"She wants to be friends with you and Jamie?"

Ruth shook her head. "My friend," she said. She cast a sorrowful glance toward her brother. "She says Jamie is going away soon, just like Daddy."

Martha didn't plan it, or even think it. It was an automatic reaction and one she regretted instantly. Her hand snapped out, fingers wide, and slapped her daughter across one beautiful cheek. "These are not things you say," she hissed. "Ever. Ever. Do you understand me?"

Tears welled in Ruth's eyes but didn't fall. She stared defiantly, even angrily, at her mother. "I thought you wanted me to tell you. You asked me."

"You're making things up," Martha said. "Mean things."

"I'm not," Ruth said. She stuck out her lower lip. It trembled for a moment then the tears came and she ran back toward the house.

Jamie stopped swinging. "Aren't we going?" he called across the yard.

"No," Martha said. "Not today." He hung his head, but didn't complain. Something in her chest shifted, lurched, and she reached toward him, willed him to come and tuck himself into her arms. He looked so fragile. He pursed his lips, frowned, and then turned away from her. He sat on the swing, facing away from the house, giving little kicks so the swing moved in tiny, slow arcs. Later she heard him on the phone, talking to James. "I miss you," he was saying. "I wish I could come to see you." He was quiet, listening while James spoke. Then he said, "All right. I understand."

That night it rained, and sometime in the night the rain turned to snow, and when Martha awoke the backyard was frosted white. The snow was piled in miniature drifts of tiny sharp crystal flakes on a shocked-frozen landscape of brown stems of grass and dandelion leaves, each encased in translucent shell. She was fixing coffee, feeling the thickness in her head begin its retreat just in anticipation of caffeine, looking out the window as she measured the dark grounds into the filter basket, amazed at the way the lawn sparkled in the dawn light. Something caught her eye, a dark place in the field of silver, and then she was distracted by the sound of **feet rushing down the stairs.**

Jamie thundered into the room, exuberant as she had not seen him in months, it seemed, or even a year. This Jamie no longer seemed pale to her; he was exquisite. His eyes were dark and fierce against his milky skin, his fair hair shone in the thin morning light, casting silver in the same way the blades of grass encased in ice shimmered on the lawn. Behind him came Ruth, bouncing with excitement, reaching out as if to touch Jamie but then pulling back as though at the last minute too shy. Or timid.

Jamie threw his arms around Martha and she was instantly ashamed of the strange fear that had welled up in her when she'd seen him. The thought that had come unbidden – like so many of her thoughts – to her mind: that isn't Jamie. Not even he; that.

"Look, it snowed!" Jamie shouted, arms still around her. "I want to go outside; can we? Can we please?"

"Let us go outside," said Ruth. "He wants to play!"

Martha held Jamie's shoulders and moved him back away from her, looked down into his dark eyes. The glittered at her, black as raven's eyes, then she saw they were only the strange and beautiful gray-green eyes she'd looked into so many times before. She pushed all of the other things that were nagging at her back, as far back as she could get them, and then smiled at him. "I love you, Jamie," she said.

He laughed and then he and Ruth capered in the living room while Martha poured cereal into two bowls for them and cut up an apple into slices. The meat was soft, the skin beginning to wrinkle a bit. It was too long since the apple had been plucked from the tree, a week too many in the warm kitchen.

After they all got dressed and went outside. The sun had already freed the grass from its casing of ice and melted most of the tiny flakes of snow. Ruth clambered onto a swing and began to pump her legs, humming to herself in rhythm. Jamie stayed close to Martha, following her as she circled the yard trying to remember what it was she'd meant to do.

"I'm glad we're here," Jamie said abruptly. Martha stopped and turned. He was standing with one shoulder touching her side, gazing up at her. His eyes were dark, deep. He smiled. Martha looked up into the blue-gray sky and saw the snow was beginning again, tiny peppering flakes. She smelled the frost in the air and the smell of wood smoke and suddenly she remembered what she'd meant to do. It was the smoke that reminded her – recalled for her the day she'd planted the bulbs. The day Jamie had cut his hand in the woods.

The day he cut his hand? she thought. Is that really how I remember it? Her mind presented her a snapshot of the young policeman who'd come to the house that day. The unacceptably perfect young man.

"Like I said, lots of boys tell stories like this one; have been for fifty years, a hundred years around here."

But he was wrong, she thought. Then with a shiver. And he knew it.

She shook her head. It didn't matter. Nothing mattered except that James was here. Jamie was here. She meant Jamie was here. And Ruth. And they were a family.

She walked, with Jamie hugging her side the whole way, to the place where she'd planted the tulip bulb the October before. The ground was dug up, thrown up, really, as though what had displaced the earth had forced it from below, not pulled it from above. The raw earth in the hole was a dark, rusty color – like there was iron in the dirt, she thought, or blood.

As she stood staring at the hole, she caught something else of out the corner of her eye. A barely perceptible, now that the frost had begun to melt, trail where the grass lay pressed down, as though something had been dragged across the lawn in the middle of the night. Dragged from the house to the woods. And perhaps she only imagined it, but tiny footprints next to it as well.

"I'm glad we're here," Jamie said again, this time his voice only a whisper.

Martha saw an image in her mind then – she imagined Jamie, not the robust, healthy Jamie standing next to her on this crisp October afternoon, but a frail, drained Jamie, naked and ghostly pale, someplace deep in the earth, as cold and dark and dirty as a dungeon. He was hunched there, arms about his knees, and he was crying. Around him stood a legion of little old women, bald head wrapped in black mantles, each round face fleshy and wrinkled, as pale as the white of an eye. Each of them with a shining pair of golden scissors – scissors that cast the only light in that whole dark place. "Mama," Jamie said in the vision.

"Mama," Jamie said, and she started because she hadn't expected the voice next to her, but far away, rising from some infinite depth.

She turned her gaze down to him. His eyes were dark and wild with some emotion that would have looked like glee if the rest of his face hadn't been so solemn.

"Aren't you glad we're here?"

Inside the house the phone began to ring. James. She expected Jamie to turn, to sprint for the door, the way he usually did when his father called. He stood silently next to her, looking up into her eyes. A faint smile flickered over his lips and he laid his head against her hip.

"Yes," she said through lips growing numb in the settling cold. "I'm glad we're here."

◇◇◇◇◇◇◇◇◇◇

Ernesto Burden is a husband, a father and the vice president of digital media for The Telegraph and related sites. He is also a writer, a runner, musician and an avid student of the Web, technology, literature and religion.

Love And War
John C. Caruso

Yeah, you think that's bad? Well, I've got a dating nightmare for you. This happened back while I was in med school at Brown.

Med school is this weird sort of incestuous little club where people mix and match all over the place. You don't have time to meet anybody who's not in your program so you end up just dating guys from your classes or your study groups or whatever. Before I declared Pediatrics as my specialty, before I even met Jason, I dated this one guy in the program for about three weeks. Alex was your classic tall, dark and handsome -- you know, Eastern European macho-type guy. He kind of looked like that Goran what's-his-name from ER, that sexy doctor they added after Clooney left the show.

Alex was super smart and the sex was just completely mind-blowing. He was more demanding in bed than what I'm used to and I really dug that. He knew what he wanted and wasn't timid like American guys. Just between us, it was the most passionate sex I've ever had in my life, though in retrospect, I suppose passion is overrated.

I think it was President's Day or something, and we decided to drive down to Newport and stay at a little B&B. The weather's totally cold that time of year but they have the Newport Winter Festival down there, and we had a great time looking at the ice sculptures, and doing the city-wide scavenger hunt, and going to the Chili Cook Off. I don't think Alex had ever had chili before, and he definitely couldn't handle the spicy stuff. It was hilarious because he got all red in the face and sweaty. His nose was dripping and everything, but he was way too manly to admit when something was too hot for him. He made up for this weakness later when we went to the Martini Contest. I'm telling you, those Slavs can drink anybody under the table. I think vodka is like water to them. Sunday night, I had too many martinis, and Alex practically had to carry me back to our room at the B&B.

The next day on the drive back up to Providence, I had such a terrible hangover that I kept getting car sick. I had to make him pull over off the highway a couple times so I could walk around and get some fresh air.

After one of these little walks to clear my head I got back to the car and Alex has the radio on and he's sitting there behind the wheel jerking off. I'm surprised, so I get in and I'm like, "What, didn't you get enough this weekend?"

He glances at me and says, "No, it's this story."

So, I listen to the radio and he's got NPR going with some report about how the Serbians have been running these prison camps where they rape Bosnian women they've captured. And the women aren't just used as sex slaves. They get pregnant from being raped by all these Serbian guys and they're forced to have the babies.

"You want to help me out here?" Alex asks.

I just look at him, like he can't be serious.

"You could suck me off or something? Make yourself useful."

I'm like, "No thanks, I think I'll wait out here."

He just shrugs and goes back to work, ignoring me and focusing on the business at hand.

I get back out of the car and stand there in the cold, looking at my own breath in the cold air. I can't believe he's actually in there beating his meat while he listens to that story about these horrible, horrible war atrocities. But he's totally getting off on it.

When he's done, I get back in the car, and we try to make small talk the rest of the drive back up north.

I was half afraid he would turn into a real asshole when I tried to break up with him, but after he dropped me off, I just didn't call, and he didn't either, which was a relief. Our paths haven't crossed since, and I'm glad, though a few months later I heard that he declared his specialty as OB/Gyn.

◇◇◇◇◇

Shroud 4   The Journal of Dark Fiction and Art

***

HIRAM GRANGE?

www.hiramgrange.com

Coming soon...

***

D.L. Snell's Market Scoops

Unprecedented Insight Into The Publications That Are Shaping The Modern Genre Fiction Market

NOTE: *Author D.L. Snell conducted the following interview to give writers a better idea of what the editors of this specific market are seeking; however, most editors are open to ideas outside of the preferences discussed here, as long as they fit the basic submission guidelines.*

THE MARKET

* Anthology: Dark Jesters
* Editor(s): Nick Cato & L.L. Soares
* Pay rate: $40 +copy
* Deadline: 30 November 2008
* Description: Novello Publishers is seeking 10 hysterical stories to fill their first trade paperback humorous horror anthology. (More in guidelines)
* Submission Guidelines: www.novellopublishers.com

THE SCOOP

1) What authors do you enjoy and what is it about their writing that captivates you?

Gary A. Braunbeck's writing always digs deep inside me and resonates on levels I (usually) didn't know I had. Tom Piccirilli never fails to satisfy, and his ability to write in nearly any genre fascinates me. And although at times his novels can become routine, Bentley Little's macabre situations keep me coming back all the time. He's been my favorite for quite a while now.

2) What are your favorite genres? Which of these genres would you like to see incorporated into submissions to this market?

Horror, comedy, and bizarro. While Dark Jesters is a humorous horror anthology (which covers the first two genres), I also find that a surreal, strange tale told from a humorous angle can be great if done properly.

3) What settings most intrigue you? Ordinary or exotic locales? Real or fantasy? Past, present, or future?

I'm more into present-day stories, although I'm open to anything. One submission we received takes place in the Stone

Age and it's one of the best we've received so far.

4) Explain the type of pacing you enjoy, e.g. slow building to fast, fast throughout, etc.

While I like a story that kicks into high gear from the first paragraph, I'm more concerned with Dark Jesters that the story maintains a consistent "aura" of humor throughout. That can be done in a subtle way as well as rocket-ship style.

5) What type of characters appeals to you the most? Any examples?

The average Joe. One of the things that make Jeff Strand's Andrew Mayhem series so good is Andrew's just an ordinary guy who manages to find himself in insane situations. Most of his stories use similar characters. Most of his stories work!

6) What is your policy for vulgarity and sexual content?

I'm not a fan of profanity, especially when it's overused. Swearing in every sentence weakens its effect, and in humor, makes the author sound like he's still in junior high. While I understand most people don't share this view, I find the writer is forced to be more creative with their humor by relying on situations and ideas rather than an abundance of vulgarity (I mean, Andrew Dice Clay is funny, but after 15 minutes his shtick gets played out).

For Dark Jesters, sex is fine depending on how it's used: I don't find rape funny, and if an author does I'd rather him/her not submit to this one. But a story with little to none of these two elements has a better shot (and remember, that's MY view: my co-editor L.L. Soares is a fan of the extreme stuff, so I'm sure we'll have to come to agreements on a couple of stories).

7) Horror and violence can be blatant or suggestive. Which one do you prefer and why?

I've always thought suggestive violence works wonders: I grew up in the late 70s/early 80s watching films like Dawn of the Dead, Friday the 13th and all the euro rip-offs and slashers that came with (and before) them. Yet despite my love for gore (at the time), the scene in Al Pacino's Scarface--where his brother is chainsawed in half--freaked me out more than any horror film (such as Pieces) that actually showed the violence. That scene, to this day, is hard to watch, and you hardly see anything. I've read a few stories where implied violence blew my mind (such as Gary Braunbeck's incredible short, "Need," from the Corpse Blossoms anthology; by the midpoint of the tale, when I realized what the mother was up to, I actually felt my stomach drop. That's powerful writing).

8) In fiction and in life, what do you find most horrific?

As a parent, I can say anything dealing with children. There's been some great novels and novellas over the last several years that deal with missing children, abused children, etc., many of which were very well done. Other than that, I live in New York, and like most other New Yorkers I have a feeling that something (whether it's a terrorist attack or a natural disaster) is inevitable. These scenarios usually keep my eyes glued to the pages, where I hope they stay.

9) In general, do you prefer downbeat or upbeat endings?
For this anthology, whichever enhances the story (i.e. makes it funnier).

10) What are the top three things submitters to this market should avoid?

1. We've received a bunch of zombie stories the first four days of submissions, so we're quickly becoming tired of them (although one was fantastic and will most likely make the final cut).

2. Several submissions were way below the 1,500 minimum word count. We're really looking for the 2K mark, but anything from 1,500 – 2K will give the submitter a better shot.

3. About half of the subs were nowhere near being a humorous HORROR story: if someone sends in a humorous tale, but it's NOT horror-oriented, it makes me wonder if the submitter even read the name of the anthology.

11) What commonalities are among the stories you've rejected? Is there a particular aspect authors seem to get wrong?

Besides the zombie thing mentioned above, most of the stories we've rejected felt like build-ups to bad punch lines. We're not looking to publish an anthology of "jokes." If anyone is interested in how humorous horror is done right, get your hands on some Joe Landsdale, Jeff Strand, or any of the authors that have been published by Novello Publishers. There are also other presses (such as Delirium and Skull Vines Press) who put out some good, funny horror.

12) If you reject a story, how open are you to a revised version, or do you only want revisions upon request?

We only want revisions if requested, but any rejected author is free to submit another story.

13) Describe a story you've recently accepted or short-listed. What made it stand out from the slush pile?

We short-listed a couple, but the one that's most likely going to make the final cut featured both intelligent and "loony" humor in the action scenes, and did it all in great taste---yet it's still undeniably a horror story.

14) What trait are you seeking most in submissions to this market?

If you can make me and L.L. Soares laugh, you have talent (especially L.L., as he's a part-time simian comedian). My dream is to (one day) release one of (if not the) funniest humorous horror anthologies--whether it be this one or a future edition (we plan on making Dark Jesters a series, possibly every two to three years). Make us laugh--make the story as funny as you can. AND keep it in a horror-story setting.

15) Any last advice for submitters to this market?

Follow the guidelines. Sounds simple, but as most editors will tell you, few people take the time to do it.

For more scoops, go to marketscoops.blogspot.com.

100 terrifying New England tales for reading or retelling around the campfire. Completely original stories of the American old country from some of today's masters of modern horror. A collection unlike any published before--a resource and a source of hours of thrilling entertainment. A dark Yankee treasure!

ORDER AT WWW.SHROUDMAGAZINE.COM

Random Shots:
Tim Deal and Author Michael Laimo at Context 21

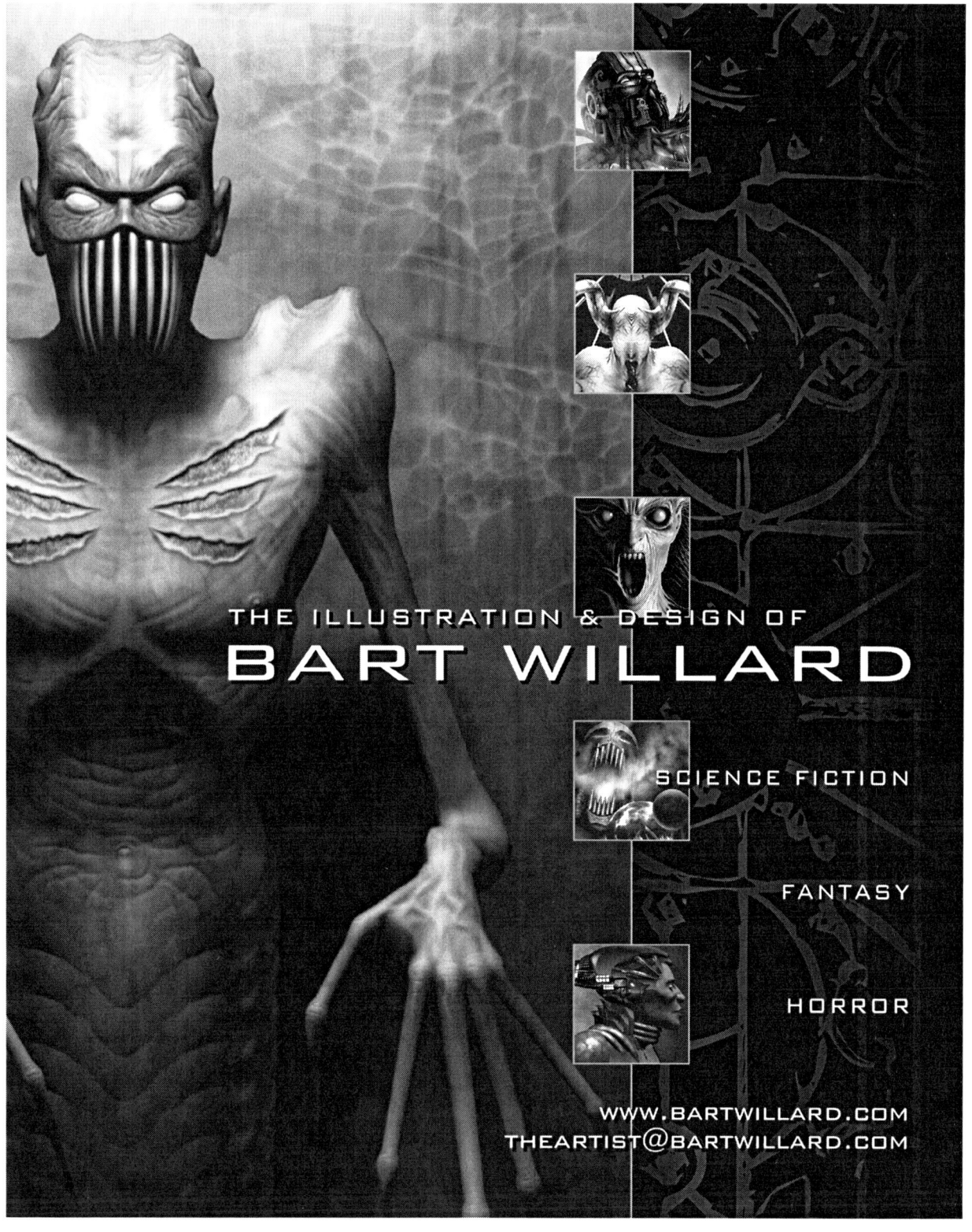

Shroud 4   The Journal of Dark Fiction and Art

SHROUD SPECIALTY PRESS SHOWCASE:
INFERNAL HOUSE
By Norm Rubenstein

Each issue we will be highlighting one of our Genre's newer Specialty Publishers and allow them to acquaint themselves with our readers. This issue we introduce Infernal House (IH). Norm recently sat down with Larry Edwards, Publisher of Bloodletting Press, and along with Shane Ryan Staley (Publisher of Delirium Books), the co-owner of both The Horror-Mall and Infernal House. The ilusatrations are from Alex McVey for Brian Keene's *Darkness At The Edge Of Town*.

Norm Rubenstein: What are its aims and goals of Infernal House?

Larry Roberts: There are really four main areas of small press horror publishing. The first is what I would call "General Horror," which I would classify such imprints as Bloodletting Press, Delirium Books, Necessary Evil, Cemetery Dance, etc. Then you have the old reprint presses like Ash-Tree Press, Midnight House and Tartarus Press. Third, you have the trade paperback or POD publishers. Lastly, there are the high-end exotic binding type presses like Charnel House, Lonely Roads Books, and Centipede Press. With over sixteen years of publishing experience between us, Shane and I both felt that it was time for us to throw our proverbial hats into this high-end book-collecting arena. Our intent with this imprint is to produce heirlooms that will be passed down for generations and enjoyed by collectors for many decades to come. We want our books to be the focal point of the most discriminating collectors' libraries.

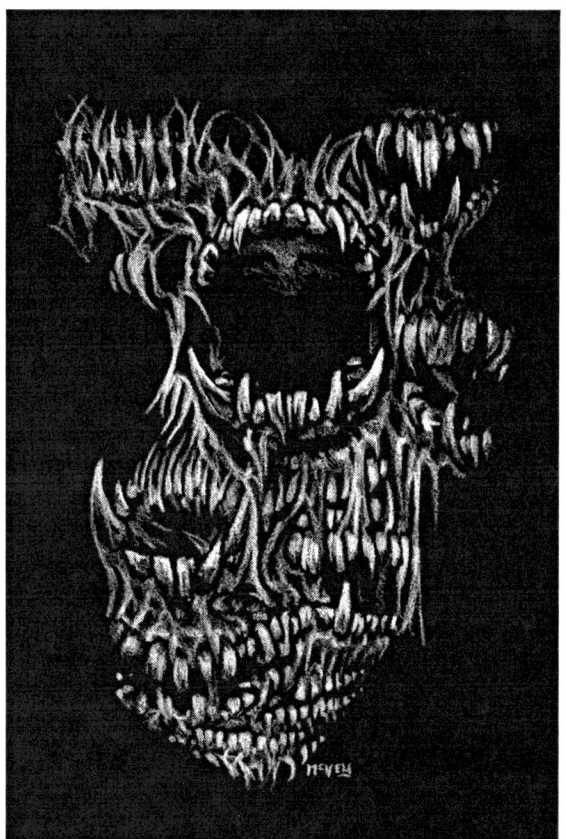

Norm Rubenstein: How andwhy did you and Shane Staley come up with the name "Infernal House"?

Larry Roberts: Shane and I went through about 200 different names and Infernal House just sounded right to us. We both felt that "House" rather than "Press" gave the imprint a higher quality feel, which is exactly the intent of the imprint.

Norm Rubenstein: I know that IH's inaugural title is Brian Keene's *Darkness At The Edge Of Town*. Was there any specific reason that you and Shane decided to pick this particular title to start IH off with, and is there anything about the book's content and construction that you would care to share?

Larry Roberts: The Infernal House imprint will only be publishing what many would term A-List authors, and only original content. Brian Keene filled the bill on both these requirements, and we liked the concept of the plot so much that we felt it would be a perfect title to start our new imprint. I can't get too much into the actual book because we want it to be a surprise when it lands in collectors' hands. I will say this though; the book will be unique in both its interior and exterior. Shane did some unique things with the layout, and in all my years of collecting and publishing, I've never seen an interior layout quite like Darkness on the Edge of Town. I believe that the collector will find it a unique and exotic book from the binding to the very last page.

Here are just a few of the specifics on Darkness on the Edge of Town
· Archival paper stock.
· Handmade French marbled endpapers by the renowned artist Lucy Lapeirrie.
· 16 full bleed illustrations by the very respected artist Alex McVey (See above)
· Full page signature sheet.
· Rice paper will cover all illustrations.
· Binding and slipcase of the limited edition will be in Moroccan leather.
· Lettered edition binding is top secret at this time, but let's just say its material will be very exotic indeed.
· Unique Tray case for the lettered will also be bound in very exotic materials.
· Lettered edition will come with a hardcover chapbook by Brian Keene that will never be reprinted, and have a completely different signature sheet.

Norm Rubenstein: Is there anything concerning IH's future and titles that you can share with the SHROUD Magazine readers?

Larry Roberts: Our next title after *Darkness on the Edge of Town* will be *Haunter of The Threshold* by Edward Lee, which Lee promises will be the most hardcore book he's ever written. All those who have read Lee's work know just what a bold statement that is.

Norm Rubenstein: Anything else that you'd like to say or share with the SHROUD readers?

Larry Roberts: I hope that SHROUD readers will stop by Horror-Mall.com and check out all the books we offer for collectors.

◇◇◇◇◇◇◇◇

Norman Rubenstein is a retired litigation attorney and judge. During the 1980's Norm negotiated a character merchandising agreement with the British Broadcasting Company relating to their DR. WHO television series, and produced a number of Conventions, (one of which was featured nationally on the Entertainment Tonight TV series). Also a line of merchandise relating to DR. WHO. He subsequently co-produced ten theatrical productions throughout the United Kingdom including one that ran on London's famed West End for six months, and produced a premiere of an A. R. Gurney play in Chicago, IL that starred George Segal and Betty Buckley. Norm now writes a regular column "Macabre Musings" for Fear Zone, and reviews books and films for Horror World, The Centipede Literary Supplement, and the Horror-Mall, and is also the Literary Reviewer for the Pod of Horror. Norm is currently at work co-authoring his first screenplay, a Horror Genre story, of course. Norm can be reached at norm@macabremusings.com.

TEMPLE
GERARD HOUARNER

Claire tended to the altar with alarming ineptitude, distracted by gems in the kylix she called the offering plate while pouring the day's fresh wine into the ritual ram's head rhyton, nearly knocking over the tall, red-figure amphora worth more than the Manhattan penthouse condominium that was their home and work place. Their Temple.

Claire. Fresh from the academy for fatherless sisters. Her beauty was eternal, a forever Spring.

Sarah had been that beautiful when she arrived at the Temple. But she'd been older. Experienced. Reverent and respectful. This one was too young. She hadn't finished her training, probably should not have been recommended for higher service. But the Temples needed hetairai. Even as they were being destroyed, the needs of the devoted still had to be fulfilled. Or else, they'd all be lost forever to the gods.

The security guard standing at his post in the vestibule, his crisply tailored suit only slightly bulging, couldn't keep his gaze off of the young girl.

Sarah stayed by the floor-to-ceiling window, letting Clair finish her obligations, no matter what the risk. Her own devotions to the ash tree, its shadow sprawled across the stone patio tiles, its endless phalanx-ranks of golden spear-head leaves brilliant in the Fall mid-day sun, wound down to their habitually fading appeals for guidance.

No one was home. Something to do with the shallow root system confined to a complex hydroponic support system disconnected from the earth 40 stories up. It was a miracle the thing was alive, at all. Like so much else, the tree was a symbol: of power, the past, dreams of the future. Like the antiques. No one visiting the Temple treated the stunted freak of a tree as if it was real. Just like the women.

The sun was low in the Southern sky, sinking to its Winter Solstice. She missed Summer.

The rhythm of changing seasons pushed her closer to a precipice she did not want to approach. A sadness shadowed her of things passing from her grasp. She felt like the little girl she'd been when she found Yiayia, white hair frayed, bony hands splayed like crushed dead spiders on the table, tea cup shattered on the stone floor, dead among her precious olives. And she'd thought, no more stories, no more hugs, no more knowing winks as she went off on the school's morning hike or sat, exhausted, her head filled with secrets and the screams of visiting maenads, watching the sun set on another day of miracles.

Claire hummed a popular song from the radio, a series of lurching phrases more rhythm than melody. Sarah shivered. The loneliness of her life smothered her, just like when she'd taken the ferry to the mainland for the last time, knowing all that she was leaving behind was gone from her forever – the old monastery where she'd been raised and tutored, the rocky hillsides and the hidden spring with its lone guardian who loved all the girls who came to draw water from its source, the songs of blackbirds in the morning, yellow scorpions dancing on her palm, the festivals and plays and plentiful almonds, figs, and pistachios at the town plateia. She'd waved at sponge fishermen in their boats beneath the hot sun scattering light across the waves in a carpet of restless diamonds. They'd looked away, warding curses with quick fingers, denying her the comfort of a simple glance as they worked, leaving her alone with the future captured in the bloody soreness between her legs.

The downstairs buzzer rang. The guard answered, spoke to the doorman, told Claire her appointment had arrived. The young girl went to her room, leaving Sarah to greet their visitor.

Being around someone so young

made her think of the retirement she faced, mourning the dead she did not know.

The guard let her answer the door, but stood in the hidden alcove, weapon drawn, watching the security screens. The attacks always came through the front door, but the Temple didn't want to intimidate their visitors with too obvious a show of security. A flicker of disappointment passed over the grey-haired gentleman's face when he saw Sarah, but she smiled, pretended she didn't recognize him from their past liaisons, and led him to Claire's room. And then she went to shower, feeling at last that the sperm of her own recent visitor sprayed in and on her had finally died, cold and unfulfilled.

* * *

He wasn't a hero, or even a companion. Just another spear-carrier tattooed with the trophies of hard-fought victories: scarred face and hands, broken nose, cauliflower ears. Compact, muscular, he reminded her of a shadow she'd seen when she'd walked the Labyrinth with the other academy girls, in the company of would-be heroes reciting ancestral tales of epic murder. The field trip's matron caught her going after the shadow, or else she might have tried seducing a left-over monster so she could kill it with an honest blade and earn the right to attend a different kind of academy, where children had, and could become, proper mothers and fathers.

And more.

What the heroes did never seemed so difficult to her. Let the heroes try doing what was expected of her and see how well they did.

The man was gentle, uncertain, careful not to hurt her. His days were over. When he was done and gone, a voice on the intercom asked her a question. She looked to the surveillance camera, shook her head and said she never once feared for her life. She gave back a portion of his tip toward his funeral.

* * *

The dark shape flickered at the periphery of her vision. She turned. Nothing there.

The gods again. Passing by, checking in. Lurking. Trying to influence the world. Searching for a path back in to the places in which they'd lived, the hearts they'd once called home. But they'd been pushed out by other spirits singing in mechanical voices, buzzing with an electrical hiss.

They didn't leave messages, anymore. Maybe they spat on the old altars. Their time was done. They were ghosts paving the way for worshipers tending barren trees and hollow temples.

* * *

The hard, flinty man inside the soft shell of a body gave her sloppy kisses as he groped her body with the sense of entitlement that came with secret knowledge accompanied by very little truth. Where were the mass murderers when you needed them? she asked herself.

He came as soon as she reciprocated, and then she spanked him and had a proper go at his real pleasure, as she always did.

"Tell me," he whispered, when they were done.

"You are a great man who will die in the company of your peers," she answered, and he was satisfied. She didn't bother with the details of cold tiled floors and walls, fluorescent lighting, and liquid food.

When he was gone, no one questioned her through the intercom. Truths didn't change, unlike secrets. Or illusions.

* * *

Sarah didn't have orgasms with her visitors. Pleasure came to her through the old ways. She enjoyed the foreplay of rituals: preparing, mixing and burning the herbs, fungi, poisons and animal parts. They relaxed her by bringing her back to simpler days on the island.

Made her ready for ecstasy.

The Temple was more than a place for sex. To most visitors, their intercourse was as important as what was revealed in their union. But truth was too often blurred in lust's satisfaction. In the end, truth didn't matter. Getting off did. Which was as good an explanation for the fall of gods, old ways, and their followers, as any other.

The truth was, the sex never gave her pleasure. No man or woman ever reached deeper into her than the smoke to which she surrendered when she made special offerings to the gods. The gods were silent, but the visions clear. And more profound than the ones she experienced when johns fucked her.

She wasn't an oracle, but she wished, if she couldn't be a killer, that she'd been given the opportunity to follow that path.

She'd trained with the young oracles, briefly, as she and the other academy girls had at the camps of heroes, priests, artists, and all the other remnants from ancient times. Temple service required well-rounded and cultured servants who understood all possible visitors.

In the caves, and the ruins buried underground, she'd danced with the figures painted into murals, the statues of gods and goddesses, shadows, spirits, ghosts. One told her he was Homer. Another, Jason. Even dead, men lied.

She'd breathed deep from smoke rising from primal pits, learned how to make her own, to ride the curling, rising, drifting ribbons through the air, into herself, dipping and diving, riding through wonder and doubt, until she was ecstatic with the unfolding of ever-changing possibilities and free from the chains of certainties.

All to weave crude spells of sweat and strokes, piggish grunts and withering cries, that revealed nothing more than banal paths born from pain leading through life and death, wealth and power, poverty and defeat.

She still had the smoke. It took her elsewhere, through games she'd learned as a child among the oracles, eluding the matrons and guards, shifting and sliding and whirling through cracks and crevices, finding the quiet, lost corners where no human breath had ever been taken. Sarah still dreamed that she was a goddess, chased by a mere mortal, playing with the arrows he fired at her, so ignorant of what he was hunting. And when she'd run too far ahead and lost her pursuer, she met another child, this one half-animal, half-human, who showed her teeth and claws and the blaze of wild eyes. "Our father was mighty, once," the creature always told her, challenging her to run away as a small pack gathered in the shadows.

But instead of running, screaming fear, and letting herself be eaten by them, she used what she'd learned of the Temple ways to make love to them, each one in turn. And in the bloody future she saw in and through them, she found all the pleasure she'd never find in the world of flesh and mortals.

There was her ecstasy. And since she survived, she assumed her dream lovers found what they needed, as well.

* * *

The man with false hair and a slight paunch came once a week at the same time. She took his briefcase and gave him a martini, helped him to the sofa. They watched baseball games, old ones when the season was over, smoked cigars, drank beers, and argued over Hall of Fame candidates.

The voice on the intercom always asked about him. Sarah said the man was still going places.

* * *

"Do you think the Erinyes are back?" the security guard asked.

They talked, sometimes, when they'd been on Temple duty too long and became accustomed to the beauty to which they were exposed. Sarah hated being polite with them. It wasn't part of her work. She didn't want to be normal. But the cameras were always on, and anyone could be watching, and she wasn't ready to mourn, so she answered civilly, "Our own curse come back to us."

"Can the gods be far behind?"

"An end of times, and a new beginning. The gods clearing out the old, making way for the new."

"Yes. That would be an explanation."

"Was another Temple attacked?"

"No."

He told the truth. She'd done her own research. It was against the rules, but how was she supposed to see the future and the fulfillment of everyone's destiny through her cunt if she didn't keep informed?

Spanking, she'd learned from her inquiries, was the new thing. The old thing made new.

Athens had been first. Everyone slaughtered, torn apart. Power and communication cut, even wireless transmissions scrambled. Recordings ruined. Bodies unrecognizable. Extra ones tossed in – homeless, tourists, terrorists, as if to salt Temple ground with common blood. It worked.

Lisbon, too.

In Hong Kong, there'd been a fight. The guards were better. An agreement had been reached with the Tongs; they'd been fighting for millennia without stop. But they'd gone down.

Los Angeles had proved the most dangerous. The police arrived before the followers. There had been a crime scene investigation. Officials had gone as far as announcing a cult murder orgy. Manson, all over again. Madness.

The Temple's true nature, and the trail of the followers leading back to ancient times, remained uncovered.

All thanks to the gods. Or to California.

Perth had been pathetic. The attackers had time to arrange the bodies, spelling out ancient curses in blood and entrails.

They always came through the front door. Like old friends.

The johns? The guards? The priests?

Maybe it was time to get out of this business. Leave the Temple. Follow nothing. But what would she do? She couldn't read her own future. What would Claire see if she went to her? What would the voice on the intercom ask?

She didn't need answers from strangers.

She never wanted children. A husband. She never wanted anything for herself. Sarah was good for what she'd become, and probably nothing more. The truth to herself, she was not really a hero. The only real question was, had she become everything she was good for?

"Do you see anything?" the guard asked.

For a moment, Sarah wasn't certain if she was being propositioned. "Why don't you ask the oracles?"

"They're blind. Cut off from the real world. Useless. You're in the flesh of it. What do you see coming?"

"I can't see anything, either."

But the guard's questioned stirred curiosity about what was happening. Why attack only the Temples? Were old gods truly coming back, or new ones rising? Was there a rebellion surging through the ranks of followers infected by the buzz and crackle of modern times? Was she too old-fashioned to have been invited?

Was Claire going to kill her?

Despite the cameras and the guards, she slept uneasily that night.

* * *

A hard night of harder men, relentless, smelly, intense and brutal, distracted her from threats to the Temple.

Each man was overwhelming, possessed by a lust that brought their interaction to the verge of rape. They must have been raised like wolves, she thought, and found their omega, the one they could safely abuse, in her. Next time, she'd try direct them to Claire.

As the men continued with their business, Sarah looked out window at pair of hawks circling in the sky, rising, then vanishing southward above the sky-scrappers on their seasonal migration.

Already, she knew the voice on the intercom would have nothing to ask about the men. Just as the pack had nothing to ask of her.

* * *

Sarah noticed Claire consistently drew the old ones. She got more of the young ones. They were wearing her out.

Smoke and dreams helped only for a while. She couldn't stay under the influence for long. She spent time at the Temple altar and the ash tree, performs the necessary rites and prayers, purifying herself, cleansing her vision, searching for guidance, a direction.

Is this all that I'll do? she asked. Waste my flesh, crash it against the harsh shores of these men? I'm not the sea. I'm the one that gets worn down, not the rocks.

In the mirror, she saw the sadness of death corroding her beauty, destroying her power over men and women, her usefulness to the Temple. Would she stop being able to glimpse destinies? Would memories , names, beliefs and truths all slip from her grasp, tumble over that terrible precipice, until at last she'd have nothing else to do but get up and follow them all over the edge to see where they'd gone, and try to recapture them in death?

Sometimes she wondered what would happen if she cut off the genitalia of a man who visited her and tossed them into the sea. It was an old tradition, though one usually passed between son and father. Would his daughter be born from the waves? If she carved open the top of a man's head, would his daughter jump out? Is that how she'd been born, and why she'd been sent to the academy for fatherless sisters? What ever happened to her mother?

Just because they were fatherless daughters didn't mean they were motherless.

* * *

Her eleven o'clock arrived. Middle of the day. A lunchtime quickie, so he could go home to the wife and family in the evening, on time, washed of guilt.

He came, and she pretended to anoint his pleasure with hers. The gods were invoked. The ceremony was complete. Would his prayers be answered?

She saw only blood.

It could only mean an early death.

* * *

"What do you see?" her four o'clock asked. Young, unassuming. A foot soldier.

"Nothing." She told the truth. Visions didn't come if there was nothing unusual coming. He was too small. In more ways than one.

"I'm too big for you."

She laughed. "You flatter yourself."

"No. You see the ghosts of gods, and fountain spirits, and the fate of men who've come inside you. Little things. Pathetic. They don't matter. You're too small to see me coming."

A foot soldier with delusions of grandeur. This is what the followers had come to. "Do you ever miss not having a mother?"

Surprised, she said, "I had a mother, but we were never introduced. But no, I don't miss her."

"I don't either. How about a father?"

"No." Not quite a lie. It was the status of having a father among her kind that she missed.

"Fathers can account for much. I know. I knew my father. He mattered."

Maybe what the conversation needed was a dash of western-style therapy. Then he'd finally jump out of bed. "Did he hit you?"

"No. He raped my mother, then he killed her and ate her, and tried to do the same with me."

Delusions again. The boy sounded old, older than he should.

"Who are you?"

"Thank you," he said, finally getting up. "For everything you've done. Thank you. And I'm sorry. I've already started."

The voice on the intercom didn't ask about the boy after he left. The guard checked the young man's records and found everything in order. Just another soldier visiting the Temple.

Sarah stared at the camera in her bedroom, then walked to the intercom and played with the talk button. She didn't even know if she could summon anyone with it. Only the intercom at the entry was connected to the downstairs lobby.

But she had nothing specific to offer. And boys like that weren't her problem. Boys like that were the responsibility of priests and teachers and elders. And the gods.

Let them do their jobs as well as she was doing hers.

* * *

She woke at two in the morning to the sound of someone sloppily eating in the living room, where dining was not allowed.

She came out in her robe.

Her four o'clock was sifting through Claire's entrails, as if reading them. His naked body was more muscular than she remembered, no longer a stripling youth's, with hair she hadn't noticed before. Compact, coiled like a cat ready to spring. His suit, shirt and tie were draped neatly over a lamp, shoes at the base. He looked up and gave her a bloody smile. "I see your death," he said, then laughed.

She didn't.

There was no where to run. The downstairs guard lay against the front door, the upstairs guard across his lap. She checked the cameras. Still there, but no doubt dead. No one had come to break down the door.

Her eleven o'clock sat up on the couch, next to a woman Sarah assumed was his wife. She was impressed. A homeless man sat in the recliner, an older woman with a Henri Bendel shopping bag still in her hand lay sprawled on the carpet outside the bathroom.

"The doorman would have been too easy," she said.

The man stopped laughing. "The neighbors, too. You have to work to create mystery. And awe. The work of gods is not easy." His fingers had turned to claws. Horns protruded from his head, which transformed before her eyes into a cross between a bull's and a wolf's.

Old legends. They changed in detail, depending on the storyteller. And here was proof everyone had missed the gods' joke of a hybrid beast. A simple bull man hadn't been good enough.

His musk scent quickly overcame the stench from Claire's ruptured bowels.

"Get out while you can," Sarah said.

"Don't pretend to be one of the Erinyes. It doesn't become you. Your fatherless kind aren't killers. Mine are."

"You're from the Labyrinth."

The man-turned-beast sat back. His cock lay flaccid along his thigh. "Long ago. Heroes conquered there. We only came back to remember the horror of our births. Not for revenge, or even a taunt. There was no fight in us. We were ghosts of the past, forgotten, invisible.

"But you saw us. And you met us truly when you came to where we were hidden. Caves. Ruins. Where we'd waited for thousands of years, not men or beasts, just children without destiny or purpose. The gods left us behind. Or forgot us. We raped and killed and fed, like our father. But through accidents – lost visitors, ship wrecks. Never proper sacrifices. You Temple girls were always so carefully guarded. We never could touch you.

"But you sought us out. Came to us in vision and in flesh. We asked if we were going to live or die, and you said yes. You gave us a future. You set us free."

A faint flicker of pride illuminated the precipice on which she stood. So close to the edge, she thought. How easy just to surrender, to fall over. And yet, she'd done something great with her skills and talents: awakened the past. What hero or priest could say the same? "Where are the rest of you?"

The beast patted his belly. "Inside me, now. I was best at following my father's ways."

"You're the last."

"The first."

"The Minotaur, broken out of his Labyrinth."

"I'm more than the thing that was my father. The world is my Labyrinth."

He stood, went to the kitchen. With the largest of the knives he'd found, as well as his claws and brute strength, he began rendering the bodies and scattering their remains throughout the apartment. He pilled the severed, mutilated heads atop the altar. Splattered blood across the walls, ceiling and floor. Smeared feces on Claire's bed.

He pointed with a butcher's knife to Sarah's bedroom.

"Why the Temples?" she asked. "Why not heroes descended from the one who killed your father?"

"That one saved me, and my brothers, from our father's appetite."

"The legends never mentioned children."

"Illusions made by men." He gestured with the knife, again. "The truth earned your heroes my gratitude. I'll go after them when I'm done with all the rest, when I've taken the comfort of their Temples, the wisdom of their elders, the hope of priests, the future of their families, and nothing is left of the old days but the heroes. They'll appreciate that kind of death."

At the beast's approach, Sarah backed into her bedroom. She stared into the creature's sunken eyes, past the blade and the teeth. She didn't recognize him from her dreams. Like the rest of the followers, she'd been living on, and in, the past. And just like the followers, she'd obscured what she hadn't forgotten, leaving her to live like a fool in a dream world as far from truth as any of the Temple's visitors.

"If I'd known you were here, I would have saved this place to be the last Temple I took," the beast said, cutting loose the robe from Sarah's body. "In gratitude for your awakening me."

Sarah bowed her, withdrew to the bed, lay down smoothly, like a dancer, in a single continuous motion. Like water, flowing from fountain to another.

On the sheets, she writhed, and turned her head, eyelids fluttering, and opened herself while coiling arms and legs around a missing body she seemed eager to embrace.

The beast snorted.

He was, at heart, still only a man.

Sarah wove her spell of surrender, the way so many men liked it, the heroes in particular, and the priests, so eager to master what they could not know. The slightest moan, the sweat breaking on her brow, the glistening pink between her thighs, all gathered like threads into a tapestry of seduction, just like she'd been taught.

The beast grunted as he jumped on the bed. With a roar, he drove the knife into the headboard, then laughed at the gesture. His breath was hot and bloody. He was hard and ready.

He came down on her, and she wrapped herself around him. This wasn't like any dream she'd ever had, or any man. If this was the same creature she'd met years before, through oracle smoke in hidden caves, then their encounter really had changed him. She would not have survived such a meeting then, any more than she could now.

Sarah grabbed his horns, screamed, made him rise and take her with him, and a small part of her still thinking understood why his kind would be considered bull rather than wolf. Size mattered.

She took the pain, catching the glint of surprise in his gaze. How many of her sisters had tried riding the bull? None. They would have had to do more than scream.

There was no point to kissing or touching. The monster was aroused as much as she could take. All that mattered lay between her hips. She moved, remembering the smoke, the freedom of dreams, and for an instant the beast seemed to remember, too, his first time with a woman who'd reached into him, awakening hunger for more than survival. He paused, staring at her, through her, at the destiny she'd given him.

Sarah stretched. Backwards. Placed her hands on the knife handle. Held on, tight. As if she held her life. Let the next spasm jerk her forward, tearing the knife out of the backboard.

The blade came down in an arc ending at his throat.

The beast saw the blade at the last instant before striking. Moved. Too late. His destiny had arrived.

She rolled away from him, breathing as hard as she ever had racing along rocky hillsides under a blazing sun as part of her training. Her hips felt as if they'd been dislocated, her spine was on fire, her guts a greasy mass about to erupt from her mouth.

The creature still breathed, chest heaving, as he lay sprawled across her bed. Blood bubbled from a wound deep in the base of his neck. He was ready, as she had been, to surrender. For some reason, he couldn't find the knife embedded in him. The claws kept scratching at his jaw.

She pulled the blade out. He was bleeding out on to the sheets. His throat was bare for the cutting. Heroes bragged about chopping off the heads of monsters. It was the only way to know for certain that a thing was dead.

Was she a servant in the Temple? A killer?

Or something else.

She went to her private bath, took a quick shower, keeping an eye on the fallen monster, the knife in her hand. The beast moved a leg. Her heart jumped. He wasn't dead, yet. But he wasn't ready to start the fight over.

Sarah packed a bag with clothes that wouldn't draw attention to her, picked up weapons and ammunition from the guard's station, money and treasure from the safe and the bloody altar.

She went back to her bedroom, showed the beast the knife, and let if fall.

He snuffled, struggled to rise, couldn't. "Live?" he asked.

"Do what you have to do," she said.

"My future?"

"Still waiting for you."

"You don't care?"

"I've seen the future."

He started to speak, his lips moving, but stopped, uncertain. His eyes roved in their sockets. He might die, anyway.

"They'll be here soon," she told him. "You'd better crawl away or they'll finish you. At least this Temple is done."

"I'll find you."

"Is that what you think? I'm leaving the Temples, and all the rest of it. You'll never find me. Neither will they. I'll be in the places all of you fear, the ones you never come to. I'll be with the common people. The poor. The dirty and filthy and stupid. And I'll see you coming. I won't be caught next time. And when I see you coming, I'll kill you."

"When did you become a hero?"

"If I was a hero, your head would be my trophy."

"What are you?"

"What the gods wished you'd been, but none of you could ever be."

"I hate riddles," the beast said, managing to roll over, and off the bed. He landed with a crash that wasn't as loud as his size promised.

Sarah kept going, refusing to look back and confirm that her young boy was back, gouged and wounded, ready to assume the role of sole survivor of the Temple's assault. A good trick. Slow her down, get her back to him and close, turn her into the final casualty while he used his status to get in deeper among the followers.

He'd have to tell them she'd been carried off.

"Tell that to the sphinx," she answered, and left him, the apartment, and all the she'd ever known.

There was no ferry, this time. Only questions: what would a man be like. A real man. Or a real woman.

Something, anything real.

What gods refused to answer, she would.

◇◇◇◇◇◇◇

Gerard Houarner has had a great many short stories and a few novels published over the years, many of which play with mythic elements. His latest novel, *Road From Hell*, has its roots in Indian and African religions. His collection/anthology *Dead Cat's Traveling Circus of Wonders* and *Miracle Medicine Show, w/ GAK*, is based on Egyptian myths.

During the day, he workd at a psychiatric center in the Bronx.

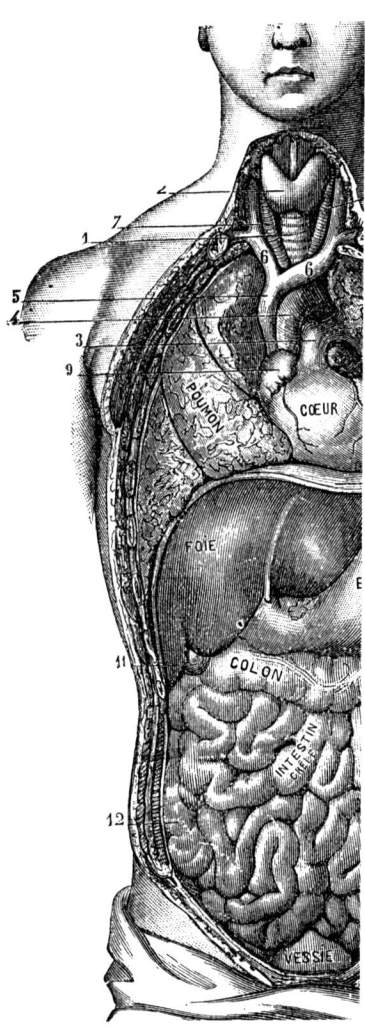

Flash Fiction Contest Honorable Mention

Alone
Edward Fleming

Josh drove silently down the dirt country road; the tires, slowly rolling over the leaves and gravel, were the only sounds to be heard. He parked the car just off the road, killed the engine, and then walked out into the cool September air.

He made his way around to the passenger's side and opened the back door, grabbing a shovel, tool bag, and a small leather satchel; he made his way to the grave site some fifty yards up the hill.

He stood before the grave of Mrs. Joshua Hanson, a Swedish immigrant who had died during childbirth in the winter of 1853. Her husband remarried and moved to Pennsylvania the following summer, leaving Mrs. Hanson to rest alone for eternity. Josh knew the history of the grave from his online research.

Since his daughter died six years ago, Josh had become some what detached from society, spending most of his time alone on his computer. Little Amanda was everything to him; then, in the blink of an eye, everything was gone.

The wind howled as the moon played peek-a-boo through the cloud cover. Josh stood above the grave; he plunged the shovel into the earth and began to dig. About an hour later, and only four feet down, his shovel found the old wooden casket. Using a pry bar, he lifted the lid.

Mrs. Hanson lay peacefully, her tattered dress draped over her dirty bones. Josh reached inside the satchel, pulled out a small vial of liquid and a thin black notebook. He opened the book and read a page-

long passage. Then, reaching down, he slowly poured the liquid on the corpse.

Hoisting himself out of the hole, Josh made his way back to the car. He fished the keys from his pocket and proceeded to unlock the trunk. There, bound, nude and terrified, was Carlos Vega, a twenty-four-year-old convenience store clerk.

Josh grabbed his victim and lifted him out of the trunk. Draping Carlos over his shoulder, he made his way back up the hill. Carlos convulsed violently, trying in vain to free himself as he gazed upon the open grave. Josh lowered his shoulder and dropped the clerk into the casket.

Carlos had never met Josh before that night, and Josh hadn't spoken a single word during the whole kidnapping. Now, standing over the casket, Josh spoke for the first time.

"I think you need to spend some time with older women."

Josh replaced the casket lid and began to pound the nails back down. In an instant, Carlos Vega, registered sex offender, understood exactly what this was about. As the first shovelful of dirt fell on the casket, Carlos felt something shift inside his tomb. He froze as he felt the bony arms and legs of the corpse start to embrace him. Silently he started to sob as her cold dead hands began to grope and grab him in the darkness.

◇◇◇◇◇◇◇◇◇

Shroud Submission Guidelines

Fiction: Shroud considers horror, dark mystery, dark fantasy and suspense short stories up to 5,000 words. In addition, we are interested in tightly woven flash fiction, and (in some cases) serialized novellas. Thriller and Suspense tales with a horror aspect are also welcome. We HIGHLY recommend that you buy a SAMPLE ISSUE in order to get a clear idea of our style and tone.

We are especially interested in:

Mythic horror in a real world setting; Classically-themed horror and suspense; Supernatural horror; Creature horror; Dark Fantasy in a contemporary/RW setting; Noir with a horror element.

We are LESS interested in:

Hard Science Fiction; Sword and Sorcery or anything set in a fantasy world; Stories about serial killers; Vampires ala Rice; First person accounts.

Submission Format: Send us electronic submissions in .DOC or .RTF format as a file attachment. Your subject line should clearly say "SUBMISSION". Simultaneous submissions are NOT okay. Please do not send us multiple submissions -- please only send us one story at a time and do not send your next submission until we give you a reply to the first. Reprints are fine provided they have not been published within three months and the author currently bears the copyright. A short bio would be nice, including any awards or published credits, however your story will stand on its own merit.

Response Time: Averages 2 to 4 months, but stories kept for further consideration by the editors may take additional time.

IMPORTANT: If you have NOT received an acknowledgment of receipt for your SHORT STORY within 1-5 Days of your submission then it is likely the submission was formatted incorrectly. We do appreciate your hard efforts and your creative vision, but with more than 350 submissions a month, if your submission is incorrectly formatted then it will be (unfortunately) deleted... sorry.

Artwork: Please query with samples. We are actively looking for talented artists for covers and B&W interior illustrations.

Nonfiction: Looking for well-researched stories on supernatural phenomenon, dark music, art, and interviews of key players within the genre, film reviews, game reviews. Query first. Payment .02-.03 cents a word.

Payment: Rates of .02 (most) to .05 (very few) cents per word, plus one contributor copy. Payable within 30 days of publication. Up to 5,000 words; maximum payment of $250. All rights revert to the author upon publication.

Anthologies: We automatically consider all fiction submissions for our active anthologies. If accepted, Shroud pays .01 cents a word plus two copies of the published collection.

Send To: editor@shroudmagazine.com

Novels and Novellas

Submission Guidelines (continued)

Shroud publishing is interested in building a catalog of intelligent dark fiction novels and novellas. If you have a COMPLETED manuscript or a series of short fiction, please query with a short synopsis and one sample chapter. Send to the editor.

A note on novel and novella submissions: we are a small press. We have a small press budget. If we are able to put your novel or novella into print we will do our best to market and distribute it, but the likelihood of you or us getting rich is very slim. Consider long and hard before you submit to us. We do not offer advances and our royalty rates will be modest. Having said that, if accepted, we will edit, design, layout your book, get it printed, sell it direct, and do our very best to get it distributed through a major distributor. WE will incur all of the aforementioned expenses, not you. We will never charge you for reading or publishing your book. Nor should you ever be.

So if this works for you, we'd love to see your novel/novella.

Response time for novels/novellas could be 3-6 months as our reading time permits.

***

For more information about Shroud please visit our Website at:

WWW.SHROUDMAGAZINE.COM

See our publications, join our forums, send suggestions, and more.

***

Made in the USA